DESERT BLOOD

"Look out!" Cameron Black yelled. "Take the ones on the left!"

Five Apaches had begun a charge toward them. Black two-handed his Remington and triggered off. His first shot took an onrushing Indian in the leg and he crumpled. Cameron switched his sights and got off two shots. One went wide and the other found flesh. The brave swatted at his shoulder as if it was an insect, but blood gushed from it. He dove to the ground and Cameron lost sight of him as the brave disappeared in the red dust.

LONE TEXAS RIDER
Owen G. Irons

PINNACLE BOOKS
WINDSOR PUBLISHING CORP.

PINNACLE BOOKS

are published by

Windsor Publishing Corp.
475 Park Avenue South
New York, NY 10016

First printing: May, 1991

Printed in the United States of America

One

The warrior was too bold. He took the dead man's scalp and held it high, the sunlight glinting on the blade of his scalping knife. Cameron Black shot him. The bullet from the Remington .44 stopped the proud Apache in his tracks as he performed his death dance and he too fell to the desert sand to await the coming of the vultures.

Cameron jacked another round into the breech of the rifle and waited, thumbing perspiration from his eyebrows.

There would be more Apaches out there. Just now he felt grateful to them. The dead white man had been trying to kill him as well, and had come damned close.

The desert was an empty sheet of rippled white, the sun beating down. He saw nothing of the Indians, nothing of the dark riders who had been following him since Alamogordo.

There was a brief stalemate out on that merciless desert, and if Cameron Black could make his move now it was just possible he could escape from the Apaches and the gang of whites as well.

He looked to his gray horse which stood in the hollow, head hanging with weariness; then in a crouch he moved to it and knowing there was nothing left to lose he heeled it hard and the big gray started off at a run toward the broken country beyond the sand dunes.

From somewhere a shot was fired, but it came nowhere near the tall man. He simply lowered his head and kept riding.

They were back there still, temporarily pinned down by the Apaches, but they would be coming on. They had followed him too long to give it up now.

But who in hell were they! And why did they want his blood so badly?

He shook the canteen hanging from the big gray's pommel, knowing how long it was going to last. Reluctantly he let it hang where it was and rode on through the brilliant daze of the day, letting the gray work its way over the rocky maze and nopal cactus.

It was all so far from Nacogdoches.

Beneath the Arizona sky his thoughts drifted back to his Texas days, the days before he began to ramble—the days when he had no killers on his backtrail. . . .

The Rafter B ranch was working only half a day. At noon the hands began to wash off the dust, to brush out their good clothes and shave for the party at the neighboring McCulloch ranch.

Winter was coming on and there was time for one last Indian summer dance, and that was what Susan McCulloch had planned.

"Cameron!"

Cameron Black turned his head to watch his brother

6

ride up to the door of the barn. He was still mounted when he came through, walking his horse to where Cameron Black was working.

"Better start getting ready, hadn't you?"

"Dad wanted the buggy all spiffed up. I've just about got it now." He nodded toward the yellow-wheeled buggy, its body brightly cleaned, the leather seat freshly saddle-soaped.

Simon Black tilted his hat back and leaned forward in the saddle as his smart little sorrel cutting horse blew through its nostrils and backed a step.

"I remember when he used to ride old Shadow, just sitting up there so proud. When we were kids, that was the proudest moment—Dad letting me ride along on Shadow."

"They were good days," Cameron agreed. Now the old man was crippled up and old Shadow had been turned out to pasture.

"Tomorrow? We going back to work on the house?"

"Yes," Cameron answered. "A man needs a place to take his bride, and winter's coming fast."

"All right. Has Susan seen it yet?"

"Not yet. She knows what we're doing, but I won't take her by until it's finished."

"I'll have Finny lay out your gray suit," Simon Black said. "One thing—Carroll and Hecht already are hitting the hooch. They told me they wouldn't, but I can smell it a mile away."

"I'll talk to them," Cameron Black said with a frown. "I won't have them ruining Susan's party."

"Carroll still hasn't forgotten that whipping you gave him—you should have fired him then."

"I guess you're right, but he's a good hand most times,

and they're hard to come by out here."

Carroll and a man named Tyler, who had since drifted, had been caught taking some calves from Rafter B, branding them with their own iron, and pushing them into a pocket valley in the hills. It wasn't unheard of—that was how some of the biggest ranchers in Texas had started—but Cameron Black hadn't been willing to tolerate it. He and the big blond man had gone to it with fists and feet and teeth until Carroll had agreed to mend his ways.

Hecht was no prize either. He had drifted in out of nowhere with his guns and his constant bottle. Sullen and dangerous, still he did his work, and as Cameron Black had said, good hands were hard to find. It was necessary to have men with some fiber in them in this country where Comanches still rode and raiders from across the Mexican border struck occasionally, so Black had overlooked their too-obvious shortcomings.

"I'll keep an eye on them," Cameron said, and his brother, touching the rolled brim of his hat, backed the cutting pony smartly from the barn.

Cameron's father was already dressed. The old man sat stiffly on the faded sofa he and Cameron's mother had had shipped all the way from Boston. His gnarled hands rested on his cane. The collar of his shirt cut his neck sharply. The black suit was loose on his shrinking frame. Once there had been bulk to Adam Black's shoulders, depth to his chest, and iron-hard muscle in those arms. Now he was old, knew it, and disliked it intensely.

"You're looking fine, Dad," Cameron said as he entered the dim parlor.

"For a walking corpse," Adam said, his silver mustache twitching. "Only reason I keep this suit is so

8

y'all will have something decent to bury me in."

"I don't like you talking like that," Cameron said, removing his chaps.

"Why not? It's true. A man lives, a man dies. I've done the one and now it's gettin' close to the other." In a less contentious tone he asked, "Where's the girl?"

"Susan?"

"Who else? Hell yes—Susan McCulloch."

"Getting all prettied up, I expect," Cameron answered. He took his spurs off and hung them on a hook on the wall, then took off his rough-out work boots.

"You ought to marry her," the old man said.

"That's the idea, Dad," Cameron said—was his mind starting to slip? "I've asked her, she's agreed, her ma and pa have agreed. Simon and I are building that house up on Snapping Turtle."

"Only bright spot around here. It's dust and decay, Cameron. That girl shows up and the house is filled with her singing and good cooking. Y'all ought to hurry things along, have some babies. The little ones . . . so full of juice and excitement, not like an old bastard like me."

"There'll be kids," Cameron answered. "I promise you that. Soon as the house is done, we're getting hitched."

"Should move her in here," Adam Black complained. "Need something lively and young around here."

Cameron cleaned up and shaved. His gray suit had been laid out on his bed by Finny, the houseman and cook. Dressing, he looked in the mirror and wondered again why a woman like Susan McCulloch would want a lanky, dark-eyed, dark-haired, curly-haired coyote like him. He supposed he looked presentable enough and so, placing his new Stetson on rakishly, he walked stiffly in his new boots to where his father waited impatiently.

9

"I'll drive the buggy, Dad . . ."

"You'll ride! You're a Black. Just get me onto the seat of that woman's rig and I'll drive myself to the McCulloch ranch."

Cameron grinned. The old man's pride hadn't diminished since he had ridden west after the War Between the States to carve out a ranch from the raw, Indian and white raider-infested land. He expected his sons to have the same pride. Only a town man would ride a damned buggy; a man sat the saddle.

Simon, looking trim and eager in his black suit, had arrived and together they took Adam to the buggy, placing him carefully on the seat while he fussed and complained more about age.

Then they rode out westward toward the McCulloch spread, Carroll and Hecht following, Finny coming last aboard his squat white horse.

Finny was another odd one. He seldom spoke, sang in Gaelic, carried no weapon. Irish, he had no drinking habit they knew of, almost always wore the same red shirt and faded jeans. He had weepy eyes, deep blue and faraway. He had certain quirks—did not want an "e" placed in his name to make it the more usual "Finney," objected to anyone touching his cutlery, and hated dogs.

Carroll had now broken into song. He was blond, bearded, big across the shoulders. He was drunk.

"Shouldn't have let them tag along," Simon Black, riding beside his brother, said.

"Could hardly tell them not to come," Cameron answered. "No sense building resentment. None of us has had a break since roundup."

"Might mean trouble."

"We've seen trouble," Cameron Black answered, and

10

they rode on across the scattered sage flatlands toward the McCulloch ranch. Cameron's thoughts were already far away from Carroll. He was thinking about the little strawberry blond ahead.

"Maybe the widow Phillips will show up," Simon said wistfully. He was scratching thoughtfully at his chin.

"Last time you didn't even ask her to dance," Cameron Black said.

"No, I ain't the hand you are with the ladies, brother; all the same I'd like to look at her. A man's only a man, isn't he?"

"Yeah." Cameron looked at his brother, knowing his feelings, that restless, constant urge a man gets. He had felt that way before he had known Susan. He wished there were more women in the area, but they were few and widely scattered. "You'll come across a good one someday, Simon," he said.

"Sure." Simon Black grinned and fell silent.

Carroll was still singing and now he passed the bottle to Hecht. Adam Black turned his eyes on them and told Cameron, "Watch 'em. Watch 'em tonight, Cameron. They'll need to have a clamp thrown on."

"Then we'll do it," Cameron said, and his father, looking at his long, competent son, figured he could.

They trailed into the McCulloch ranch house yard in midafternoon. Carroll and Hecht, worn out by the hot sun and alcohol, rode silently now. Finny halted by himself in the shade of a cottonwood and walked toward the punch bowl the ladies had set up, nodding silently to anyone who greeted him.

The McCullochs' hired hand, a slim, jittery Mexican named Garcia, came out to take the reins to the buggy as Simon and Cameron Black helped their father from it.

11

Susan was there, on the porch, wearing a white dress with a blue ribbon around it. She waved to them all and then came down to hug first Adam Black and then Cameron, giving her hand to Simon.

They went up onto the porch to greet wiry old Satchel McCulloch and his plump wife, Rebecca, sat Adam down in the shade, and then began to visit with friends they hadn't seen for months; to listen to the fiddle player tuning up; to wave to the cowhands in their best clothes walking with ladies on their arms; to sip punch, steal a sip of whisky now and then from Satchel McCulloch's kitchen jug; to watch the kids playing and teasing; to look at the sky which was threatening the party, but looked like it would hold off until morning with bad weather. It was still warm, and Cameron had his fiancée on his arm. The band was striking up and the Chinese lanterns had been lighted. It was a warm, friendly, comfortable evening, with the liquor gradually warming blood, the scent of beef roasting in the barbecue pit and that of fresh biscuits from the kitchen drifting across the yard.

It wasn't until after dark that the trouble began.

Two

It was Carroll, predictably, who started it.

He was drunk, staring hungrily at Cameron Black and Susan as they danced beneath the Chinese lanterns of the pavilion. What thoughts passed through his mind it was difficult to tell, but when he turned away suddenly, he lurched into a man named Dan Schaeffer, a Rocking Double A hand. Schaeffer, reading the dark mood in Carroll's eyes correctly, was careful to apologize. Carroll was having none of it.

"You ought to get out of a man's way," Carroll snarled.

"I tried," Schaeffer replied, trying to smile. He was a mild, slender kid with his hair slicked back on this evening. He must have been twenty but looked more like fifteen.

"You ought to try harder, boy," Carroll said.

Susan McCulloch gripped Cameron Black's arm above the elbow. "Don't let him do it, please!" she said. The band had stopped, the dancers had halted in their tracks. Simon Black was standing on the porch, tilted slightly forward, undecided.

13

Carroll was in the kid's face now, his whisky breath and red eyes terrifying the unarmed ranch hand.

Carroll took the kid by the shirtfront and lifted him toward him. His right hand was cocked back but he never threw it at Schaeffer.

Cameron Black caught the arm from behind and spun Carroll toward him and as Carroll released his grip on Schaeffer and turned to level Cameron, Black's fist landed flush on the drunken cowhand's jaw, spattering both of them with blood as it split to the bone.

"I'll kill you," Carroll growled and he charged wildly at Cameron Black, flailing away with both hands. Cameron stung him with another sharp punch to his eye and then dug a right into his belly, bending the bigger man double. Then, swinging from way back, Cameron shot an uppercut through Carroll's limp guard, catching him on the point of the chin.

Carroll went down and lay there writhing.

Hecht was reaching for his sidearm as Carroll started down, but the thunder of a gun from the porch froze his motion.

Simon Black was striding toward them, smoking Colt in his hand. "That was high and wide on purpose, and you know it," Simon said. "Back off, Hecht. Better lift his gun, Cameron."

Cameron took the man's pistol from its holster and winged it away. Then he stood within an inch of Hecht's red face and ordered him, "Now it's done. Now you two are done on Rafter B. Pick up your friend here and get out. It's shoot on sight next time, Hecht, and if it's me I won't be as generous as my brother was."

"You . . ." Hecht wanted to say something, to cuss back, but he swallowed it as he looked at the circle of cowboys facing him. He helped an unsteady Carroll to his feet and the two of them staggered off toward their horses.

"Sorry," Cameron apologized to the McCullochs.

"No need to be," Satchel McCulloch said, watching the two men mount and drift away. "When something has to be done, it has to be done."

When Cameron, his arm around Susan, walked to the porch, his father was beaming with delight. "Should've made him fight a little longer," Adam Black said. "And Simon should have drilled Hecht. In my day . . ."

The band started up again, drowning out the old man's words, smothering his thoughts. Susan stood by him, holding Cameron's hand as well as his father's.

Simon hadn't returned and now Cameron saw him at the corner of the dance floor, watching the widow Phillips, who was sitting on a white iron bench talking to two other ladies.

"I wish he'd get up the nerve," Cameron said. "Funny, I don't think Simon is scared of a man on this earth, but a skirt frightens him."

"He'll meet the right one, and she'll know enough to change that," Susan said.

"You want to dance again?" Cameron asked, but she shook her head negatively.

"I'd rather walk for a time, if you don't mind," she answered.

She squeezed Adam Black's hand and they started off, but the old man called his son back briefly. "Cameron," he said, "you watch those two. They'll be back sometime if I know anything of men. If you're going walking, take this."

And from beneath his coat he pulled out an ancient

15

Walker Colt, handing it to Cameron, who put it behind his own belt before leading Susan away from the party.

They walked through the cottonwoods and followed the creek, which was bright in the moonlight. Looking back they could still see the colored lanterns. The fiddle music floated through the night, subdued by distance.

They stopped and Cameron turned his woman, holding her for a long time before he bent his head and kissed her warm mouth.

"I'm losing my breath," Susan said in wonder as she pulled back. "Cameron—the house—is it nearly done?"

"Nearly. If it doesn't snow, ten days, two weeks."

"I don't like waiting."

"I don't either, but it was a promise I made you."

"We could stay with my parents for a while."

"It was a promise I made you," Cameron Black said stubbornly. "I told you you'd have your own house to go back to after we were married, and you will."

Susan nodded, kissed him lightly again, and walked on with him beside the bright river. She knew better than to argue with him. He had given his word, and to him that was that.

"I want many babies," she said without looking at him.

"How many?" he laughed.

"Just . . . many."

"Well, unless I miss my guess, you'll have many, Susan. If . . ."

His voice broke off and he took the big Colt from his belt. He had seen the man in the trees, following them, and now, pushing Susan behind him, he cocked the gun as the man began to run away.

"No, Cameron!" Susan shouted, grabbing his arm. "It's all right. It's only Garcia."

16

"Garcia? What in hell is he doing following us around?"

"He just does that. He's always followed me. It means nothing, he's harmless."

"I don't like it."

"Really, Cameron, it's all right."

Maybe so, but still Cameron Black didn't like the idea of the Mexican hand following them when they went walking. It didn't seem quite healthy.

"Maybe we should be getting back," Susan said. She was holding her shoulders, shivering. "There's a sudden chill in the air. I hope it doesn't snow, Cameron. I want that house finished, darn you . . . our house."

"That's the whole idea, woman," Cameron Black said softly. "That is the whole idea."

But the next morning as Cameron and his brother began working on the house again, the first light snow started to fall. Cameron, on the roof, looked skyward and cursed quietly. If it got heavy they would have to shut down the job.

"Hear old Ben Travis this morning, Cameron?" Simon Black asked as they worked inside the house after lunch.

"No. Concerning?"

"Says he cut Comanche sign on his spread yesterday. They took a few head of cattle and lit out for the Smoke Hills."

"He say how many?" Cameron asked, frowning.

"Three in the band he cut. No telling how many there are. In this weather, you know they'll likely be moving through toward Mexico."

"Well, we've handled them before," Cameron said,

17

but it wasn't that simply done. If it was really going to snow hard, there was too much to be done on the ranch. The cattle would have to moved out of the far canyons and pushed toward the main ranch. With Carroll and Hecht gone they were shorthanded, although Simon had hired a hesitant little man named Cherry in Nacogdoches.

Their father's house had to be looked to, wood cut, hay stored up for the horses. That would all leave little time for the house on Snapping Turtle. Especially if the Comanches were roving.

"Well," Simon said, putting a hand on his brother's shoulder, "it'll likely let up. It's early for snow."

"Likely."

Simon was looking at the four-room house, eyeing their work, the stone fireplace, the low ceilings to keep the heat in, the sanded cedar paneling and pinned wooden floor.

"I wish I had a place like this. I wish I had a woman like Susan."

"There's still the widow Phillips."

"Yeah," Simon grinned, "she's still there, isn't she? I'll have to have you give me courting lessons."

"I'll help you build your house, Simon, you know it."

"I know you would . . . for now, brother, let's get this one built."

But the weather wouldn't cooperate, nor would the Comanches, nor the outlaws.

The snow came down heavily and Cameron Black, riding the circuit looking for strays and raiders, came across the dying fire. He had been so close on their heels without knowing it that there was still a running iron in the fire.

He turned up the collar of his sheepskin coat and

18

unsheathed the Winchester.

Their tracks were plain in the three-inch-deep snow, as were the tracks of the cattle they were pushing ahead of them toward the Mexican line.

One of them must have spotted him because suddenly the horse's tracks began to show an increased gait, and here and there he spotted a steer standing forlornly in the snow, a straggler they felt too rushed to stop and regather.

Six of them, he figured. Six armed men. He reckoned his only chance was to circle on ahead of them and block their trail. He knew the country better than any of them could. This was home. He had been riding these trails since he could walk. If they kept on going the way they were they could only take Ford Pass over the broken ground, which would slow their progress, especially if they refused to abandon the rustled steers.

If he cut over Turkey Creek and made the High Ridge trail, he could get ahead of them. It guaranteed nothing—he would still be a single man against half a dozen—but it was his only chance.

The creek was running swiftly with snowmelt, and the big gray horse Cameron Black rode balked briefly, but it went through, and with the snow still falling, he doggedly rode the High Ridge trail, reaching it within an hour.

He dismounted, hitched the horse to a broken oak, and waited, searching the trail below. No one had passed yet or the snow would have been packed. He checked his Winchester and settled in behind a clump of snow-dusted boulders to watch and wait.

Hours crept by and the snow deepened, the sky going darker yet. He tucked his hands into his pockets to keep them warm. His legs, despite the long johns under his jeans, trembled with the cold.

Then he saw them.

A long line of bunched cattle pushed by riders showed as dark figures through the blur of swirling whiteness. Cameron Black smiled grimly and levered a round into his rifle's breech. He felt no compunctions. Those were his father's cattle. The old man had worked all of his life to buy them, breed them, feed them through the winters, water them through Texas droughts. These men were stealing the labor of his lifetime.

They weren't going to get away with it.

Not hardly.

Three

Someone must have spotted Cameron Black, because a hand came up and someone shouted and then they began firing at his position, the bullets flying past his head in a deadly hail, chipping at the rocks, plowing into the snow-covered ground. The gray horse reared up in surprise and fright and Cameron settled in to give them back what they were trying to give him.

The man in the buffalo coat was nearest the head of the rustled herd and Cameron shot him through the belly, watching as his piebald horse sidestepped away, tossing its head. Perhaps the horse had been tagged as well. Cameron couldn't tell, and he took no time to double-check. He switched his sights to the second man in line, a man who was colorless, featureless, making only a dark silhouette across his sight plane. Cameron shot him from the saddle and men began to scatter. Two of them leaped from their horses, others pounded away southward through the driving snow as the cattle milled and bawled and finally, free of their human guides, turned tail and started back toward home graze.

21

Still the bullets flew toward Cameron's position, but he had accomplished what he wished and had no desire to fight a prolonged battle when he was outgunned. He moved in a crouch back toward the gray horse and started it even before he had mounted, heading back the way he had come, toward Rafter B.

"The bastard," the black-eyed man in the canyon said bitterly. One of his lieutenants looked at him questioningly.

"Who?"

"Who do you think, stupid. I know who that was—Cameron Black. He'll pay yet. I swear he'll pay yet."

"At home Cherry stood in the doorway, the soft glow of the fire behind him, and as Cameron rode in and swung down, dusting the snow from himself as he walked onto the porch, the little ranch hand said, "I sent for the doctor. Don't know if he'll make it if things get worse."

"The doctor?" Cameron's face furrowed with puzzlement at first. "What for?" And then he knew and he slowly made his way to his father's bedroom to watch the old man fade away.

Simon and Cameron Black buried him in the morning next to the grave of their mother. Neither of them knew any words to say and so they just stood close together for a while before they walked back to the house, leaving their shovels in the loose earth of the mound on top of the knoll.

The two brothers sat across the table from each other, not talking about their father's death. They drank coffee and once Simon took a small glass of whisky.

"He'd have wished for Susan to be here," Cameron said.

"No way to go get her in this weather."

"No. No way."

"Finny made a rough count," Simon said, staring into his coffee. "Figures we're missing fifty head altogether."

"Guess some will be wandering back from Ford Pass."

"I guess," Simon said; then he suddenly rose from the table and went outside to stand in the snow, staring at the knoll where they had buried their parents.

It was the following night that the house burned.

The fire was burning low in the Rafter B ranch house. Simon was still out after a long day looking for strays. Cameron went out to stretch his arms, look up at the cold, starry sky, and collect some wood. It was then that he saw the smoke—too much smoke—from the neighboring ranch.

He dropped the wood in his arms and ran for the stable, mounting the gray without bothering about a saddle. He heeled it hard and lined out across the snowy land toward the McCulloch house, his heart pounding.

Comanches? Accident? Raiders? No matter, the house was on fire and as he emerged from the trees he could see from across the meadow that it was already an inferno.

Driving the horse hard across the meadow; he dismounted on the run in the yard. The heat from the house was a blast furnace against his face. Flame curled from the upstairs windows.

"Susan!" he yelled frantically, but there was no one outside the house. Flames gleamed red on the snow and he rushed to the house, kicking the door in. The rush of heat pushed him back, singeing his eyebrows and hair.

He went instead to the parlor window where the heat seemed less intense, where the flames were subdued. Wrapping his fist in his bandanna he smashed the window in and entered the room over the sill. Turning, he put the bandanna over his nose. The smoke was creeping under the door from the room beyond. The walls seemed to glow with heat.

And the small dark figure lay huddled against the floor.

"Susan!" he yelled, already knowing it was no good. Reaching her, he hoisted her in his arms. She was cold, too cold, and there was something sticky on her dress.

"Jesus!" he roared against the competing roar of the flames. She had been shot. This was no accident at all. A timber above Cameron Black creaked ominously and then began to sag, and before he had gotten her out of the window it snapped and flame fell into the room from the upper story.

His lungs were burning, he was coughing violently. Carrying her away from the house, he spoke to her constantly, but she did not respond. He felt no movement in his arms. He placed her gently beneath the chestnut tree, still talking to her, pleading with her, but she did not move.

It was then that the bastard who had done it came riding around the corner of the house on a firelit horse. He was a dark blur against the glow of the flames from the house.

In cold fury Cameron Black went to a knee and drew his Colt. He fired five times, emptying his Colt, but the man kept riding. Cameron continued to trigger the gun, the hammer falling on dead chambers time and again.

Then there was only the heat of the night and the cold

woman in his arms and the empty ache in his heart.

It was then that the wandering began.

He buried Susan beneath the tree and signed over his share of the ranch to Simon, simply leaving a note on the table. He took his saddlebags, his Remington rifle, and the big gray horse, and he rode.

He was a smith, a cavalry scout, a hired hand in turn, but her shadow was always there, falling over his thoughts, causing him to make mistakes, to grow negligent, and finally, restlessly, to just move on, running away from a ghost he couldn't shake. He was a deputy marshal in Tucson for three days before he had to shoot a man, maybe the wrong man, and he dropped his star on the floor of that saloon and again simply rode out.

He tried drinking hard, but that only made things worse.

Nacogdoches was gone but refused to go away. He met a Mexican girl in Alamogordo, but she drifted away after one of Cameron's nightmares. He stayed on, dealing cards for a living, a gaunt, deep-eyed man who spoke to few he didn't have to, who slept most of the days, emerging only at night to watch the spots of the cards, the unsmiling kings and queens pass over the green felt of the table.

"That's him," the Mexican said.

The two were standing outside the batwing doors of the Range Haven Saloon, peering in at the man in the frock coat and white hat who was effortlessly—almost aimlessly—dealing poker.

"How can you be sure?" the Indian asked.

"I'm telling you, that's Cameron Black."

"Seems a coincidence this far from Nacogdoches."

"You can call it that if you want . . . but maybe he's tracking. Ever think of that?"

The Indian nodded, but said, "He's got a funny way of tracking if that's what he's doing."

"Don't matter much, does it?" the Mexican said, turning away from the door into the New Mexico night. "He's still got to die."

The Indian nodded again. The other man was right. No matter what he was doing in Alamogordo, Cameron Black had to die. Together they slipped off the saloon walk and headed up the dusty street. There was a man they had to talk to.

It was the following night they came after him.

Four

Cameron Black opened his eyes slowly. There was still a hint of color showing in the window of his hotel room, but the sky was growing rapidly dark. It was time to rise and stare out at the anxious whiskered faces in the saloon from his wooden chair, to wonder who was going to grow drunk too soon, who might pull a gun, who would be the one to finally drill him.

Cards and alcohol are a bad combination. Some of these men would place all they had on the table and if they lost, they would go out to borrow some more. And if they lost that they would go out once more to return with a gun.

Cameron had seen all degrees of this, and he didn't like it. But he was no moral reformer, only the man with the pasteboards. All he could do was try to keep himself alive.

He swung his feet to the floor, rubbed his head, and rose. He struck a match to the lantern on the dresser and turned up the wick, looking in the mirror at his sharp, dark-eyed face.

Frowning, he washed up, shaved, and began to dress.

27

He pulled his trousers on and then his boiled white shirt—the Range Haven had a new owner who wanted his people dressed stiffly. Cameron hadn't met the man yet, but that was the word and so he had given up his soft silk shirts for the time being.

He knotted a tie loosely around his collar and then began his serious dressing.

Tugging on his polished black boots, he thrust his thin-bladed, sheathed knife in one, the long-barreled boot pistol in the other. He found his gunbelt and wrapped it around his waist, checking the Colt .44 there first. The derringer he stuck inside his frock coat pocket.

Then he formed his newly blocked black hat with the narrow silver band, and with a sigh, went out, turning off the lamp. Downstairs in the hotel dining room he ate lightly: coffee, a few biscuits with honey, nothing more. In the morning he would eat heavily after his night's dealing. He tried to convince himself, but couldn't, that it had nothing to do with an old gunfighter's fear of being gutshot with a full belly.

It was nothing but habit.

He walked outside to find the Alamogordo night warm and the town peaceful. He crossed the street as a beer wagon rolled past, and went to the stable to check on the big gray horse with the Rafter B brand. He didn't ride much anymore, and the big boy was getting fat and restless.

"He been acting up?" Cameron asked the stable hand.

"Kicking a little. Needs some exercise, Mr. Black. Want me to have one of the boys take him out tomorrow?"

"No." Cameron considered. "I'll take him for a little jaunt come morning, a mile or so to trim him back."

"What is he now, about seven years?"

"Eight. Thinks he's a colt, but he doesn't run like he used to."

"Exercise," the stable hand said. "But then, a horse gets more bottom to it as it gets older. Maybe he can't sprint like he used to, but he looks like he could be a long-runner if you needed him to be."

"Anyway," Cameron said, stroking the gray's muzzle, "oat him out. This horse has been good to me." Then out of habit he checked his saddle hanging over the stall divider, sliding the Remington from its scabbard to check the action. All useless activity, he thought. He'd either be buried in Alamogordo or reduced to hitching the big gray to a buggy . . . Thoughts of his father came back, and Cameron Black shoved the rifle back into the scabbard angrily.

"See to him," he nearly growled, and the stable hand flinched.

"Yes, sir, Mr. Black."

Outside the stable the night sounds had begun. At Madam Rose's a girl laughed shrilly. Glass broke somewhere. A dog barked and a trio of cowhands trailed up the street, pointing at the restaurant and then at the Range Haven, trying to decide which should come first.

Cameron Black crossed to the saloon.

Inside, the tinkling of Little Benny's piano became suddenly too loud. Cameron walked to the bar, and Rialto placed the habitual whisky shot in front of him and passed him six fresh decks of new cards.

"What do you think, Rialto?" Cameron asked, eyeing the crowd.

"I think it'll be a rough one, Cameron," the bartender answered. He was seldom wrong. What sort of sixth sense he had, Cameron couldn't guess, but Rialto seemed always to know.

"Then give me another," Cameron said with a brief smile, and he took another shot before he collected his rack of chips and walked to his table, the saloon girls and a few regulars calling to him or waving.

It was to be a very rough one for Cameron Black.

He set up his rack and placed his cards in the receptacle, broke out a fresh pack and ditched the jokers before shuffling them. Then he leaned back, repeatedly riffling the cards, cutting them, reshuffling until he began to draw some interest from the unshaven, dirty miners and cowhands.

Within fifteen minutes he had a full table.

He recognized none of the men around the smoky table, but that was nothing new. Men drifted in and out of Alamogordo each day. One of them was a Mexican with a flowing mustache who seemed to be folding early every hand, another was an Indian. A big man with a sandy mustache who threw down his cards in disgust each time he lost sat between these two.

None of them seemed drunk, none of them seemed to care much which way the cards fell, which bothered Cameron Black. Some men were good losers, others bad. These just did not care until the minute before midnight when the white man with the sandy mustache looked at Cameron, at his hands and then his eyes and then his hands again.

"You cheated me, friend," he said very softly, but not so softly that it didn't turn heads in the saloon.

"Don't see how," Cameron said just as softly, although one of his hands had already fallen away from the table to be nearer his holstered Colt. Now, Cameron

Black noticed three other men had drifted over toward the table and two of them were standing too close behind him.

"Plain and simple—a bottom deal," the blond man said. He took his cards and folded them in half with one hand.

"Mister, I don't need such tricks," Cameron said, placing his own cards face down on the table, fanning them out. From the corner of his eye he saw a big man with a buffalo coat ease closer. The heat of the men behind him was near enough to feel. Across from him the dead blue eyes of the blond and the black eyes of the Indian and the Mexican followed his.

"I saw you," the Mexican said.

"It wasn't too slick either," the Indian said, and then Cameron knew beyond any doubt that he was being framed—but why? What did they hope to gain from this? Money? He had little of his own. What was in front of him was in the form of chips: the house money.

"Why don't you just admit it?" the blond man asked.

"I got nothing to admit," Cameron answered. He looked past his accusers, hoping to find an ally in popular opinion. These people knew him well enough. He'd never been accused of cheating before. But there was no help forthcoming. Hell, who would want to go up against six armed men to save a gambler's hide?

"I think we should talk outside," the man with the blond mustache said, and then he flung his cards into Cameron Black's face.

Cameron's hand darted toward his Colt but arms were instantly thrown around him. A sledgehammerlike fist fell on the side of his jaw, and before he had recovered from that his chair was tipped sideways and he was spilled

31

onto the floor.

Rough hands grabbed him, a boot toe was driven into his ribs, cracking one of them. Cameron's breath gushed from his body and blood spewed from his mouth. He was kicked again and then dragged across the rough plank floor of the saloon. Angrily he kicked out at a man behind him, catching him on the knee so that the man howled in agony, but it was a futile gesture. Another fist and another landed on his face and he was suddenly out the batwing doors of the saloon and into the street.

"You'll pay, you damned cheat!" someone Cameron couldn't see through the blur of pain shouted, and he was thrown aboard a horse, which lurched forward, being led toward the river beyond town.

"What are you going to do?" Cameron asked the nearest man as they wove through the scattered pines toward the river beyond.

"Hang you, you damned cheat," was the answer.

"Who are you? Who sent you?"

There was no answer to the question. Still riding, a noose was placed around Cameron's neck. With six men around him then, with the moon shining dimly through the pines, they led him on.

"Who are you?" he repeated. His head rang, his body ached. Again no one answered. The horse moved loosely beneath him. No one spoke.

He took in slow, deep breaths, forcing himself to think, to be calm. Once they halted and tossed the rope over a limb he would have no chance at all. Perhaps now he still had a slender hope of surviving if he acted quickly enough, if he could force his confused mind to concentrate, his tortured body to react.

"I think we're about far enough," he heard one of his

attackers say—the Mexican, he thought.

They began to slow, looking for a suitable tree. They were going to hang him and he didn't even know why. There were six of them, all armed. It didn't give him much of a chance at all—but a rope was going to give him no chance.

They had been in too much of a hurry to hustle him out of town to take the time to tie his hands. A lynch mob, they couldn't take the time. The law might have shown up. That was their mistake and Cameron Black's only hope.

The man holding the rope around his neck was grinning. What he thought was funny, Cameron couldn't have guessed. In a minute he would never laugh again.

Cameron grabbed the boot pistol from his boot and shot the man through the skull. Then he heeled the horse hard, yanking the reins to his right, toward the river. A shout went up and three shots were fired as Cameron Black wove through the trees, yanking at the noose around his neck until he got it loose.

He paused, spun the horse he was riding, and fired the boot pistol twice at the nearest attacker, seeing him veer away, hit or not, he couldn't tell. Then he was into the river, riding like hell.

He hit the river too hard, finding it deeper than he had expected. The horse spilled and Cameron hit the water. The heavy current carried him downstream for a hundred feet before he could find the bottom and drag himself drenched to the bank.

A shot slammed into a tree nearby and he dove for a huge, nearly square rock, drawing still more fire. Rock fragments flew. He answered the shot, using the derringer to hold the boot pistol in reserve.

A rider—hit or shy—veered off into deeper timber.

Of the next one there was no doubt. He suddenly appeared near at hand and Cameron shot him through the heart. He fell from his mount and as he did his horse reared up in fright, but Cameron, leaping toward it, grabbed the reins and after a few moments' violent effort managed to mount.

He rode the beach hard; then when he saw what the moon showed to be a shallow ford he recrossed the river.

He was seen again. Two men from the far side of the river drove their mounts after him across the stream, their horses' bodies sending fans of silver water into the air.

A rifle cracked and Cameron, riding low across the withers of his borrowed horse, fired back and saw the rifleman go tumbling into the water. The other man kept coming, but there was nothing Cameron could do about it. Both of his guns were empty. All he could do was to achieve the pine verge, weave through it, and reverse his direction, hoping to confuse them.

He drew up in the shadow of a huge pine and waited, listening as a man passed so near he could hear the creaking of his saddle leather. Holding his breath, Cameron let him pass. Then, after a few more minutes' wait, he walked the horse forward, riding back toward Alamogordo, figuring that would be the last place they would look, hoping he was right, because a misstep now would certainly mean death.

The town was silent as he circled toward the rear of the stable, slipped into it, and saddled the big gray. His spare pistol was in his saddlebags, the Remington repeater still in the saddle scabbard, loaded.

The gray stepped out quickly, eager to move. Cameron Black too was eager to be going, away from death, away from civilization, and he moved out toward the desert as the moon rose higher and the whipping wind built.

But they would not quit. Still they followed him. With the sun a fierce red rising ball, Cameron Black saw them on his back trail and he rode on deeper into the desert and deeper yet.

And still they had come, the stalking men. Still they hunted him as the heat of the desert day fell again to night and then again was transformed into the white hot sand of day.

There was no stopping them, no eluding them until the Apaches had intervened, holding them back temporarily.

And still Cameron Black did not know who they were or why they wanted to kill him.

Five

It had no right to be there, but it was there just the same.

A broad canyon opened up to the west. Its floor was lightly dusted with gray-green grass, and here and there a bedraggled, windbattered cottonwood stood. Farther up the canyon, forms and colors that did not fit the desert landscape revealed themselves.

Cameron Black could make out what appeared to be a peaked roof and he turned the staggering horse that way.

It had no right to be there, but as he rode deeper into the canyon he could see that there was indeed a town of sorts tentatively rooted there, in the shadows of the red sand canyon wall.

Instead of narrowing, the canyon suddenly opened onto a circular, walled valley, so that the entire shape of the hidden canyon resembled a key.

The grass grew greener and higher as Cameron rode on toward the tiny settlement.

Now he could see that there were half a dozen buildings in the town, scattered apparently at random across the hidden valley's floor. The nearest of these was a colorless clapboard building, low, flat-roofed, weather-beaten.

Cameron guided the gray horse toward it.

His throat was parched when he swung down in front of the building. Both man and horse wobbled at the knees. There was a trough in front of the building and Cameron rinsed his face and wiped back his hair with water from this, allowing the horse to drink as he did so.

He had to tug the gray roughly away from the trough and tie it to the rail beside it. Then Black tramped up onto the porch and entered the building.

Inside it was dark and hot. The building apparently served as a combination dry goods store and saloon. There were sacks of flour on the floor on one side, above these were smaller sacks of sugar and coffee beans, tinned peaches and tomatoes and corned beef, blankets and boots.

Along the opposite wall was a ten-foot-long plank bar with whisky bottles lined neatly along a shelf. Behind the bar stood the woman.

She was not yet thirty, dressed in blue gingham. Her hair was dark and glossy, worn up on her finely molded skull. Her eyes were dark and quizzical, her mouth full and friendly, her body youthful and trim.

"Are you all right?" she asked with concern. Black, dusty, clothes torn, his body dehydrated, wasn't so sure, but he nodded.

"Sure."

"What'll it be for you?" she asked.

"Water. I need some water," he answered.

"We don't get many calls for that," she said with a deeper smile.

37

She watched as Black swayed and then came forward to lean heavily against the bar, bracing himself.

"You're not all right, are you. Wait here. I have to get water from the back."

Cameron nodded and hung on to the bar, listening to the woman's footsteps as she scurried away into a back room. He closed his eyes, his head spinning, and waited.

She was back in a minute with a tin cup full of cold water. Black took it with a trembling hand and swallowed it gratefully, feeling the water trickle down his parched throat, reviving the desert-dry tissue there.

He put the cup down unsteadily and watched as the woman went off again, returning with a second cup.

"Over here," she said, and Cameron followed her gesturing hand to a puncheon chair which rested in the corner of the room. There he sat with the cup between both hands, taking small sips of it, his head hanging.

Questioning eyes watched as he drank. She turned away as the door opened. Black's head jerked up and his hand dropped toward his holster automatically. She caught the movement out of the corner of her eye.

It was only a white-bearded old man who walked to the bar and said, "Whisky, Cassie. Make it two," he added on second thought.

"Sure, Byron. How's the claim?"

"Slow going, but it'll prove out. I can feel it," the prospector said confidently.

The woman named Cassie served him two shots of whisky and watched as Byron put them both down in the space of a minute, slapped a dollar on the counter, nodded good-bye, and shambled out the door, leaving Cameron Black and the woman alone again.

She came to where he sat, carrying a glass of whisky. "Here, I think you can use this too," she said, offering Cameron the glass.

"I'm dead broke," Cameron said.

"I'll start a tab for you."

"I won't be coming this way again."

"Call it a Christmas present," she said. Smiling weakly, Cameron took the glass, drinking the whisky in a single gulp.

"I appreciate it," Cameron said.

"It's all right. Do you want to tell me about it?" she asked.

"About what?"

"What are you running from?" she asked.

"Who said I was running?" Cameron answered.

"Nobody has to say it. I have eyes. That's your horse, isn't it? Not even a canteen. You've come a long way and ridden hard."

"I just got lost, that's all."

"Sure." She shrugged. "If you don't want to tell me, it's all right. But if you're in trouble, I might be able to help."

"I doubt you could help me out of this . . . why would you anyway?"

"I don't know—sympathy, maybe. Maybe I've seen a little trouble myself. Are they still after you?" she asked with intuitive insight.

Black just nodded. There was no sense lying.

"If they have a decent tracker, they'll find you here. You're exhausted and your horse is half-dead. You can't run much more."

"I can't just sit here," Cameron replied.

"That's not what I had in mind. Listen, I can help you, believe it or not. I know this area and these people—you don't. You can hole up here until you're stronger and whoever's chasing you has given up."

"Hole up in a saloon?" Cameron asked with a dry laugh.

"No. At my ranch. I don't work here. I'm just doing a favor for Gil White—he's the owner. He'll be back soon."

"They'll track me out there too," Black said. The offer, unexpected, was appealing: a place to rest, to hide out.

"No. I'll get a kid I know—the blacksmith's son, Jake Weems, to ride your horse up Rattlesnake Canyon, then release it. Rattlesnake is in the opposite direction of my ranch. They'll track it that way and eventually find the horse, but they won't find you. I've got my buckboard out back. I'll cover you with a tarp so not even anyone in town will have seen you. Then I'll drive you out to my ranch."

"I still don't know why you're offering to do this for me," Cameron said.

"I just am . . . What's your name anyway?" the lady with the dark eyes asked.

"Black, Cameron Black."

"I'm Cassie Shore. For now I want you to go into the back room and stay there. When Gil White gets back, we'll go."

"I can't repay you," Cameron said, rising to his feet unsteadily.

"Sure you can. You will. I've got a hundred chores that need doing. I've been looking for a hand anyway, but

40

not many men wander this way. First you get well," she said with a smile, "and then I'm putting you to work."

"It's a deal," Black said, and he put his hand out.

Her hand was strong but soft and Black gripped it just a moment longer than was necessary, looking into her eyes before he released it and let her lead him to a back storeroom. She closed the door and left Cameron alone in the cramped room. There was a back door but no window so he just perched on a hundred-pound sack of corn and waited in the near darkness, hoping he was not making a mistake in trusting the woman.

He was still hot, still exhausted, but the combination of cool water and the whisky had lifted his spirits and soothed his body a little.

Hours seemed to pass in the storeroom, the only sounds being the buzzing of a fly and the occasional muffled voice from the store outside. Eventually she came.

"Ready?" Cassie asked. When he nodded, she said, "Let's get going then."

She swung the back door open and stepped into the alley behind the store, looking one way and then the other before she motioned for Cameron to follow her out.

Behind the store was a buckboard wagon drawn by two mismatched, lazy-looking horses.

"In the back, hurry!" Cassie ordered, and Cameron complied.

Once he was on the bed of the buckboard she threw a tarp over him and made it fast. He felt the buckboard sway as she clambered aboard and snapped the reins, starting the horses forward.

They bumped along over rough ground for a while

41

before reaching smoother dirt—a road leading some-where. Where, Cameron couldn't guess. He could see nothing; he could barely breathe beneath the tarpaulin with the hot sun beating down.

"Whoa!" he heard Cassie yell and then the brake squealed beneath her foot as they stopped. There was a silence and then a call of hello from a young voice.

"Hello, Miss Shore," a breathless boy's voice said just above Cameron's head.

"Hello, Jake, how's everything going?"

"Just fine Miss Shore."

"Good. How'd you like to earn a dollar, Jake?" Cassie asked.

"A dollar! How?"

"Well, I'll tell you, but first you've got to promise me that you'll keep it a secret—even from your father," she said in a conspiratorial voice.

"I will," the boy promised seriously.

"In front of the store there's a gray horse. I want you to take him and ride up Rattlesnake Canyon. When you get to the far valley, unbridle and unsaddle him and turn him loose."

"Is that all?"

"That's all. Hide the saddle and bridle if you can."

The boy was hesitant suddenly. "I'll do it for you . . . but, it ain't horse stealin' is it?"

"No," she assured him, "it's not. I have the owner's permission."

"Well, I don't know why anyone would want to do that, but I will do it. And," he assured her, "I'll keep it secret."

"All right. Here's the dollar. You go and do that right now, won't you?"

"I sure will, Miss Shore," the boy vowed, and then Cameron heard the sound of running footsteps and then the snap of the reins once more, and he was being carted off toward an unknown destination in unfamiliar country by a woman he had met that very morning.

He had placed a lot of trust in Cassie Shore. He could only hope it wasn't misplaced.

Six

The ranch was small but tidy. Cameron Black rode on the bench seat beside Cassie Shore as they entered a pocket valley south of the town.

A few head of cattle grazed on the sparse grass along the narrow silver creek. In a small corral next to a low shed two horses lifted their heads at the sound of the approaching buckboard. The blue roan nickered loudly in welcome and the buckskin, curious, rested its head on the upper rail of the corral.

The house was fifty feet beyond. Very small, whitewashed, shingle-roofed, it showed a woman's touch. There were blue curtains in the windows and potted geraniums flanking the front door.

"You go on in," Cassie said, "I've got to put the horses up."

"No," Cameron objected. "If I'm to earn my keep, I'll be the one to stable them."

"You're not strong enough."

"It's not much work. I insist."

"All right," she agreed, halting the team. "They'll

back for you so you can put the buckboard in the barn."

Cameron took the reins and scooted over as Cassie Shore stepped down from the buckboard. She watched briefly as he turned the buckboard, and then went into the house.

Cameron Black swung the wagon in a half circle, lining the team, then backed the buckboard into the open barn. Setting the brake, he stepped down and began unhitching the team. He led the horses to the corral and once inside slipped their bridles and girths.

After replacing the corral rails, he walked with the tack back to the barn, where he hung the harness on the nails on the wall.

The little bit of exertion had sapped him of his strength. He was amazed at how little reserves his body had. He had always been a big strapping man, one who could tackle almost any chore. Now he felt weak as a kitten.

He looked around him at the dry hills. Along one ridge a few ragged pinyon pines stood, their limbs grotesquely wind-twisted. The small creek ran past the house, apparently having its source in a spring higher up. A few thin clouds were flagged against the pale blue sky where the brilliant sun hung. A dry breeze wafted down the canyon, gusting against Cameron Black's sweat-soaked body.

He looked back up the trail then, wondering.

Would Cassie's plan work or would they find him anyway? Had he only brought trouble to her as well? Perhaps he should have just kept riding, riding until the gray dropped, and then kept on afoot, accepting the inevitable.

Taking a deep breath, Cameron started toward the

house. The door was open and so he went on in.

"Cassie?"

"I'm here. You just sit down. Take off your boots and rest," she called from what he assumed to be the kitchen.

He did as she had suggested, tugging his boots off his hot, weary feet, sitting on a faded but clean red sofa. On the floor was a braided rag rug, and on the wall above a stone fireplace hung an Indian blanket. A wooden rocker sat in one corner. Outside of that the room was almost empty. It was Spartan but clean.

He closed his eyes, listening to the rattling of pots and pans in the kitchen, the soft humming of Cassie Shore as she worked there. He fell asleep without realizing it, and for the first time in a long time there were no nightmares.

When he awoke it was to a light touch on his shoulder, a woman in an apron standing over him. He twitched awake at first and then sagged back happily.

"Feel better?" Cassie asked.

"Much."

"A little supper and you'll feel even more so," she promised him.

"It's a long time since I've eaten," Cameron said. He stretched then and glanced toward the window, amazed to see that the sky was streaked with crimson and orange. Night was already nearly upon them.

"How long did I sleep, Cassie?"

"Probably not as long as you need to. But supper's going to be ready in ten minutes. You'll want to wash up and wake up a little before we eat. The pump is around the west side of the house. I'll get you a towel and a brush."

"Thanks. Whatever that is cooking, it's turning my stomach over with anticipation."

"Just a little pot roast," she said. "I'll get you a towel. Stand up, will you?"

Cameron shrugged, but did as the lady requested. She looked him up and down, a thoughtful thumb supporting her chin.

"Maybe," she said.

"Maybe what?"

"My father was a tall man. Not quite so tall as you, perhaps, but his clothes might fit you. I haven't got much—he wasn't much for buying clothes—but I've saved what he did have. Why, I really don't know . . . just a minute."

She went back into the kitchen and then into another room, from where Cameron heard rummaging sounds. When she came back she had a pair of well-worn jeans and a red-checked shirt. A towel was draped over her arm.

"Clean up and try these on. If they fit, you're welcome to them."

"All right, thanks," Cameron said. Taking the items he went out the front door. The evening was warm and still, the hills lost in the shadows cast by the flaming, dying sun. An owl swooped low across the meadow, making deep clicking sounds in its throat.

Cameron stripped off his clothes and worked the creaking water pump until he got a steady, warm stream of water to flow. Rinsing off in this, he toweled off and tried the clothing Cassie had given him.

The jeans were a little short, the shirt a little tight, but they fit well enough and they were certainly cleaner than his own filthy outfit. He tugged his boots back on, brushed his hair back, and returned to the house.

When he opened the door the smell of the pot roast again reached his nostrils and his stomach began to plead

47

with him, growling and tightening.

"Done?" Cassie called. "Just drop your clothes on the floor and come and sit."

He entered the little, freshly painted kitchen and saw Cassie standing near the small round table. On the table was a platter with a browned pot roast surrounded by vegetables. A gravy boat and freshly baked biscuits sat beside it. There were also a pot of coffee and two blue cups, two plain white dishes, and knives and forks.

"Well," she said, "aren't you going to sit down? Carve up that roast for us, will you, Cameron?"

She took off her apron, folded it and placed it neatly in a drawer, and sat across from him as Cameron went at the browned roast with the carving knife, slicing it to reveal the pink heart of the roast. He served Cassie two slices before she shook her head, then he helped himself.

"Don't be shy, Cameron," she said, and so he took four slices before spooning off a heap of small potatoes and what amounted to two whole carrots. He put three biscuits on the large plate and covered them with gravy. Then he settled into eat. Cassie watched him, smiling.

"I enjoy watching a man eat. If I'd known you were coming I would have made you a pie. There's an apple tree down by the creek. Dad planted it the first year we were here."

"How long ago was that?" Cameron asked.

"Six years. The man who sold Dad the land assured him that the army had the Apaches under control, that the town would flourish. Neither one was true. It seems the Apaches have the army under control—and as for the town, well, you've seen it."

"Does the town have a name?" Cameron asked.

"Sure—it's called Fortune." She smiled wryly and cut

a small piece of meat.

"What happened to your father?" Cameron asked.

"The Indians. Last year. They got three people in Fortune. One of them a three-year-old girl."

"They're still around then?"

"Oh, yes. Not all the time, but they drift through at certain times of the year."

"What times?" Cameron asked.

"Like about now," Cassie answered.

Cameron looked at her for a long minute, then got back to supper, cutting his biscuits up to go along with the meat and potatoes.

"I have to confess," Cassie said, "that my reasons for having you out here weren't all charitable. I can't handle all the work around the place. I've got cattle up in the hills I can't round up. I've got wood that's going to have to be cut before winter—it does get cold in the desert in the winter, you know?"

"And the Apaches."

"Yes," she admitted with a sigh. "They'll be coming by. They always have come by. They know where they can find cattle and horses."

"Have you ever thought of just giving it up? Moving out of the valley to a town?"

"No," she said firmly. "I won't do that ever. My father died for this land. I won't just pack up and leave it to the scavengers or the Indians."

Cameron helped himself to another slice of roast. He admired the girl's pluck and he understood her motivation, but he doubted the wisdom of a lone woman trying to hold down a ranch in this godforsaken area.

"Subtract this meal from my first month's wages," Cameron said, forking a bite of potato into his mouth.

49

"That *is* your first month's wages," Cassie said with a laugh. "Make the best of it."

When he could eat no more he leaned back, looking at the half-vanished roast, and let Cassie pour him a cup of rich, hot coffee.

"Any better now?" she asked, pouring herself a cup as well.

"Feel like I died and went to heaven," he replied truthfully.

"Those men—why are they after you?" she asked.

"I still don't know why you think someone's after me," he said, sipping at the coffee.

"If you don't want to answer, don't."

"Just a misunderstanding. A slight dispute."

"Over what?"

"They wanted to kill me; I didn't want them to," Cameron replied.

"All right, don't tell me," Cassie said, the hint of a pout in her voice.

"I'll sketch it out for you," Cameron said, and briefly he told her the story. "The funny thing is," he added, "I have the feeling that someone sicced those men on me. It's a feeling I can't explain, but it's like they were working for someone else."

"But you have no idea who it could be if that were so?" Cassie asked.

"None at all. It's probably just a crazy notion."

"Don't ignore your instincts, Cameron."

"No. A time or two it's saved my life. But I've thought this one through. I had a lot of time on the desert to do that, and I can't think of anyone who has a grudge against me. Not that kind of grudge anyway, so I guess I'm wrong this time." He pushed his plate away and wiped his mouth.

"If you're through eating, I'll clean up. Why don't you go back and rest on the couch?"

"Not a chance. I'll help you," he insisted.

"Not a chance," she echoed. "I don't want a man underfoot in the kitchen any more than you'd want me interfering with your work. And after tomorrow you'll have plenty of work to do."

"Why after tomorrow?"

"Because tomorrow you are going to spend the day doing nothing. You're not ready for hard work yet, and there's no sense in you hurting yourself or my paying you for half a job."

The lady was adamant and so Cameron just shrugged, rose from the table, and said, "I can see there's no sense in arguing with you, boss. I'm going to go outside and walk off some of this supper before it gets dark, though."

"All right," answered Cassie, already scooping up the dishes. "But if you're going out, will you check some of the ranch gear first?"

"Of course," a puzzled Cameron Black replied.

"The small pantry to the left of the fireplace," she went on "do that for me." She was putting her dishes in the pan when Black walked out of the kitchen and went to the tall, narrow pantry beside the fireplace and opened it.

In the corner a Winchester .44-40 repeater leaned against the wall, a rag over its muzzle to protect it from dust. Hanging in a warn holster was a .44 Remington revolver. Both were loaded and oiled. Cameron Black checked the action on each and went out into the twilight as Cassie Shore washed the dishes.

The evening was still warm and would remain that way all night this time of year. A horse nickered in the corral.

The first star had blinked on above the dark hills. Cameron Black slowly circled the house, barn, and corral. A breeze had begun to ruffle the trees. The last line of color was nearly gone from the sky.

And in the distance a coyote—or something sounding like one—called to the rising moon.

Seven

Cameron awoke on the couch. He had gone to sleep uncovered, but Cassie had covered him with a quilt. She was already up. He could hear her in the kitchen and smell ham frying. He got up, rubbed his head, and walked that way to find her cooking. Her hair was already done, her face washed, and she was wearing a clean brown skirt and white blouse.

She turned with a smile. "I thought this would wake you up," she said.

"What time is it?"

"Nine."

"I haven't slept that late in years," he said, stifling a yawn.

"You won't be again for a long time. Breakfast is going to be at six sharp from now on."

"That's fair." He sagged into his chair. "You look like an angel this morning."

"Thank you. You sure it's not the ham that's got you feeling so complimentary?"

"That might have something to do with it," Cameron

admitted with a laugh. "There's something about a woman in the kitchen that makes the world seem just fine."

"Is that so?"

"Sure is. That's what I always used to tell . . ." His voice suddenly broke off and Cassie, puzzled, turned toward him.

"Tell who, Cameron?"

"Nobody . . . my mother."

Cassie's mouth tightened, but she didn't press it. She came to the table, iron skillet in hand, and placed a slab of ham on Cameron's plate. Then from the oven she took a pan of biscuits, placing the entire pan before Cameron.

"What about you?" he asked. "Aren't you going to eat?"

"I told you—around here we eat at six. I've had my breakfast long ago. I've cleaned up my bedroom, forked hay to the horses, and saddled the bay."

"You're going somewhere then?"

"Yes. It's Thursday and on Thursday I always visit old Mrs. Pierce. Her husband died of the pox a few years back and she hasn't got anyone. I help her with her cleaning and, more important to her, listen to her stories."

"What time will you be back?"

"I don't know. Sometimes I stay over. If I don't make it back by dusk, you know where the rest of the pot roast is." She came and hovered over him briefly like a schoolmarm. "You make sure you do what I told you, Cameron. Rest. Eat as much as you can hold. Nap. I want you ready to work tomorrow."

"Yes, ma'am," he said facetiously. She shook her head and untied her apron. She went into her frilly bedroom, then emerged with a broad hat and a light jacket. In her left hand she carried a big old Spencer repeater.

"Mind the fort, Cameron," she instructed him. "I'll try to make it back so you'll have a hot meal. *You* rest."

He walked her to the door and watched as she thrust the Spencer into its scabbard and swung aboard the bay, unceremoniously tucking her skirt between her legs.

She lifted her hand, turned the bay, and walked it from the yard, leaving Cameron to watch, hands on hips, from the porch.

"Quite a woman," he said to himself. "Cassie Shore is indeed quite a woman."

Then he turned and went back into the house to finish his breakfast and drink three cups of strong black coffee.

By then he had already decided he was going to disobey the boss's orders. He wasn't the kind of man who can just sit around and take it easy when there was work to be done, nor did he intend to be a freeloader. It was true he wasn't a hundred percent as of yet, but he could put in some time at least.

He walked out to the corral and looked the remaining horses over.

He liked the buckskin with its deep chest and easy gait, the powerful hindquarters and intelligent eyes. Slipping beneath the top rail he approached the horse, which braced itself, eyeing Cameron Black wearily.

"Easy now. Easy big boy."

The buckskin stood its ground, not running, but looking unhappy with this unexpected attention. Cameron Black managed to put a hand on the horse's shoulder. He felt the skin shudder beneath his touch, but still the horse stood its ground. Cameron had the feeling that the horse had been well trained, but simply hadn't been ridden for a long time. Perhaps it had been Cassie

55

Shore's father's horse.

Remembering something Cassie had told him, he slipped out of the corral again and walked toward the creek behind the house.

The apples were green but sweet and he picked several of them. Returning to the corral he hand-fed one to the buckskin, which took it cautiously and then, after devouring it, nudged Cameron in request of another. Cameron gave it another, stroking its neck all the while, speaking in a low, gentle voice to it.

"That's a fine boy. Let me give the others one as well and then I'll be back with more, all right?"

The horse watched with seeming anticipation as Cameron Black again went to the apple tree. On the way back he stopped in the barn and tossed a bridle with a soft bit over one arm, tucked a blanket under the other, and hefted an old but well-tended Texas-rigged saddle with his free hand.

The buckskin was waiting impatiently. Black gave it one apple over the top rail and then opened the gate. He walked toward the horse, speaking softly again, bridle in one hand.

He fed the horse the last apple and waited while the buckskin munched it down.

"Now, then," Cameron said. "Can we try this?" And he placed the bridle over the horse's head, slipping it the bit. The buckskin fought it only slightly. Buckling the chin strap, Cameron returned to the gate for the saddle blanket and saddle.

He tossed the Indian blanket onto the buckskin's back, smoothed it, and then swung the double-cinched Texas saddle up and over. All the time he talked to the horse. It stood steady, some memory of the saddle seeming

56

to return.

He led it out of the corral, closed the gate, and with a deep breath, swung aboard, half expecting to have to break the animal all over again; but the buckskin held steady and responded to the reins easily as Cameron walked it across the yard.

"Looks like I've got me a horse," Cameron Black said to himself.

After a stop at the house to pick up the rifle and strap on his handgun, Black rode out toward the low hills where Cassie said her cattle had strayed.

It wouldn't be easy for one man to bring many home in a week, nor was there any guarantee they would stay home. But he could try. It was the least he could do for the lady.

There was little brush on the hills, only scattered sage and some sumac with here and there patches of nopal cactus, and so the riding was easy. He had time to get to know the buckskin horse, which he constantly stroked and talked to.

Cameron felt well enough, only a little fatigued, perhaps, but there was a sense of well-being in these hills. Only twice did he catch himself looking behind him out of habit, watching for the men who were hunting him.

He found the first of the cattle a mile south of the ranch house, grazing, or trying to, on scrub brush. One of them lifted its head and eyed the man on the horse with consternation.

Cameron circled the three steers and rode higher to get above them. He surveyed the land as he rode. To the south was a rocky rise which had prevented these three from wandering farther. Opposite Cameron was a sandy hill. Since he now controlled the slope to the west, that left only the narrow feeder canyon which led back toward the ranch. If he could force them into it they would have no choice but to return to home graze.

If the horse was good enough to control them.

He had no idea if the buckskin had ever worked cattle, and if it had, it had been a long time. He patted the horse's shoulder and asked quietly, "Are you up to it?"

The big horse quivered at his touch, almost as if it were eager to get to work. Whether that was the meaning of the animal's response or not, it was going to get the chance to try.

Cameron Black walked the big horse forward and now all three of the steers were watching him, their eyes wide and fearful. Suddenly Black lifted his hat into the air, yelled loudly, and, heeling the horse forward and waving his hat in circles, charged directly at them.

The cattle took to their heels.

They veered to the right and Cameron cut the buckskin that way. The horse responded at his touch and the steers were cut off. They tried then to go to the left, but again, responding to the slightest tug on the reins, the buckskin cut them off.

Yes, it had worked cattle before, and its instincts were still intact. Once more Cameron had to cut the cattle off, but soon after they were in the feeder canyon and running in their clumsy way toward home ground.

Already Cameron could see the house and in another few minutes he had them pushed onto the grass near the creek where the other cattle grazed. He drew back lightly on the reins and the buckskin halted, if not on a dime at least on a silver dollar.

He let the horse cool a little and then let it drink from the creek. Then once more they started into the hills.

They made three more trips into the surrounding country that day, bringing in as many as four at one time and as few as one cow with its calf.

It was midafternoon when Cameron decided that both he and the horse had had enough for their first day and gave it up, walking the buckskin out of the sandhills, where they had found nothing, toward the ranch house.

Topping out a small rise he looked toward the house, pleased to see the increase in the herd. He saw something else he was not so pleased to see.

There was a horse hitched to the rail in front of the house and it wasn't Cassie Shore's horse.

It didn't necessarily mean anything. Westerners felt free to drop in on friends and neighbors, and if they found no one home, to go on in and wait. Still, it made Cameron Black edgy, and he let his hand rest near the butt of his .44 Remington.

He approached the house from the blind side and swung down, ground-hitching the buckskin. Then he walked cautiously to the front of the house, pausing to let his eyes scan the yard and the barn.

Seeing nothing moving, he started toward the door.

The horse was a good one, a big black gelding with one white stocking and a white star. Its bit had been slipped, indicating that whoever was riding it meant to stay for a while.

Black walked softly across the porch and entered the house, nudging the door open with his boot toe. There was no one in the front room, so he crossed the floor to the kitchen. He still heard nothing, and that bothered him. His hand now gripped the holstered Remington.

He entered the kitchen sideways, the door at his back. Nothing.

That left only Cassie's bedroom. No visiting neighbor would go into her bedroom, and Black began to get geniunely concerned.

He drifted that way, eyes alert, body tensed. Gingerly he stepped into the room, going automatically into a crouch. The room was empty.

He poked around a little to make sure, but it was indeed empty. Frowning, Cameron Black walked back through the house, but there was no one hidden there, no message, nothing apparently disturbed.

He went outside again, peering through the rising heat veils. Still he saw nothing, no one. He circled the house, glancing toward the cottonwood trees along the creek, then crossed to the barn which was dark, musty—and empty.

What in hell was going on?

He went to the black horse which waited standing three-legged at the rail, moving not at all except when flies caused its ears to twitch. It carried no saddlebags. There was no note pinned to the saddle. It was branded with a Rocking K, a brand Cameron was unfamiliar with.

He tried to make sense out of it. Had someone come to visit and, finding Cassie not at home, gone hunting in the hills? Maybe, but the saddle carried no rifle scabbard.

He walked back down the trail past the corral, trying to read the sign, thinking two riders may have come in and, for reasons unknown to Cameron Black, left this horse and ridden out again.

He could read nothing on the hard-packed earth, however; the cattle he had been driving in had overlaid their tracks on any sign that might have been there.

There was nothing to do but return to the house. Perhaps Cassie could shed some light on it when she

60

returned. Maybe it was something so simple as someone returning a borrowed horse and tack—but then why hadn't the horse been unsaddled and corraled?

He had no clue, and guessing was going to get him nowhere. It was probably nothing. Probably.

Still it worried him, worried him deeply.

He returned to the house, took the leftover roast beef from the cooler, and sat down to dinner. And as he ate he kept his pistol on the table.

He liked none of this and he began to wonder if there wasn't yet another reason Cassie Shore had brought him out to her ranch.

Eight

Cameron forked hay to the horses and wiped his forehead with his sleeve. It was still searingly hot though sundown was near. The black horse he left at the rail, carrying an armload of hay to it. The buckskin, unsaddled, was loosely tethered in the barn, for Cameron Black had decided to sleep there on this night. To that end he had made a bed of hay covered with a tarpaulin in the back of the buckboard.

He couldn't explain even to himself why he had made that decision; there was something in the air he did not like. Recent times had made him even more wary than usual, and an odd occurrence like the appearance of the riderless black horse urged him toward caution.

Cassie apparently was going to spend the night at the widow Pierce's house since she hadn't arrived yet and the sky was purpling, a crimson slash creasing its dull violet above the rust-colored hills to the west.

He walked around the ranch one last time; his ghost rider might still, for whatever reason, somehow be hiding in the area. But he found no one.

It was still warm, a slight breeze rising with sundown as Cameron Black stood beneath the cottonwoods, listening to their rustling leaves, watching the sky go dark.

He couldn't help it. He had blocked it out for so long, but his thoughts now returned to her.

One night he and Susan had stood beneath a massive cottonwood near Nacogdoches, his arms around her waist, her eyes on his as sunset spattered brilliant colors against a cloudy sky. Light rain had begun to fall and there was suddenly a dull rainbow against the sunset. Had there ever been such an evening . . . ?

Cameron Black forced a door in his mind to slam shut and he walked back across the yard, eyes still searching. Inside the barn he sat for a long while on the tailgate of the buckboard, watching for the owner of the horse; waiting for Cassie Shore.

The buckskin shifted its feet once in awhile, but outside of that there was no sound at all in the night. Cameron was sleepy, but he would not allow himself to sleep. Again, he could not have said why, but there was something . . . something.

He propped himself up in the buckboard, and with the Winchester across his lap, alternately dozed and stared bleakly at the rising moon beyond the sandhills. The buckskin stood nearby, dozing itself.

Suddenly the horse's head came up and it stood, ears pricked. Cameron Black was instantly alert, levering a round into the Winchester's chamber.

The horse looked intently toward the yard of the house. Cameron's eyes followed those of the animal. He saw nothing but the moon and the deep shadows it cast. Then the black horse's head too came up and it looked to the west, toward the hills.

63

Cameron Black had considered briefly that the horses may have heard Cassie riding in, but with the hitched black horse looking toward the hills, he knew that was not so. Then who . . . ?

He didn't have to wonder long.

A silent shadow flickered across the yard toward the black horse. Another shuttled toward the back of the house. There were six of them in all.

Apaches.

One of them slunk toward the door of the house and Cameron placed the front sight bead on him and triggered off. The Winchester bucked against his shoulder and the night was filled with its rolling thunder as the Apache screamed, threw up his arms, and fell to the porch before dragging himself away.

Instantly the barn was under assault as the other Indians opened fire at Cameron Black's position. Bullets thudded into the planking of the barn. The buckskin reared up in terror. Black fired back three times, nicking one Apache who had foolishly tried to charge his position.

One of the Apaches had unhitched the black horse, and riding low behind its shoulder, was pounding toward the safety of the sandhills. Black had no choice but to let that one go.

To his left an Apache with a repeating rifle peppered the barn with his bullets, slugs ringing off the iron of farm implements, ricocheting wildly. Cameron took careful aim and fired once in return. The Apache keeled over backward and lay still.

Despite being outnumbered, Cameron had them at a disadvantage. He was hidden in the shadows of the barn while they were illuminated by moonlight. He tracked a fleeing Apache with his sights and triggered off another shot, and saw the Indian somersault into the hard clay, pick himself up, and hobble into the night.

It was still then, almost eerily still. The Apache he had thought to be dead was gone as well. There was nothing moving in the yard. Gunsmoke still clouded the barn, acrid and thick, and still the buckskin quivered nervously, but outside of that it seemed as if nothing at all had happened.

Except the black horse was gone.

Cameron gave it an hour more, and then cautiously, he went out into the night. He kept his back to the barn for a minute, remaining in shadow; then he began a search of the area. He found no one.

Since they knew now that he was in the barn on their first foray, he moved into the house, latching the door, taking more ammunition from the pantry. He doubted they would return, but he couldn't be too careful.

There would be no more sleep that night. He propped himself up in a chair where he could watch both the windows and the door and remain in shadow, and with his rifle across his knees, passed the night waiting.

When dawn arrived with subtle pastel shades of color surrounding a bleak, reddish sun, Cameron Black walked out of the house. The night had passed quietly but slowly. One never knew if the Indians would be back or not.

He could find no sign of the previous night's battle but a few spent cartridges. He looked toward the hills, wondering if the Apaches had drifted on or had remained in the area, hoping to collect more horses or beef from the Shore ranch.

Briefly he considered tracking them into the hills to find out, but the idea was foolish and he knew it. A lone rider on the trail of a band of Apaches might just as well stop and blow his own brains out. It would save a deal of torture.

It was three hours later that Cassie Shore rode in, waving and smiling as she approached the corral where Cameron Black was currying the buckskin horse. His sleeves were rolled up, his red-checkered shirt open an extra button, his hat perched on a corral post.

He grinned, slipped through the corral bars, and waited hands on hips for her to arrive. He took the bay's bridle as she swung down, and received an unexpected hug. She was carrying a small burlap bag.

"A few surprises for you. I saw a knife I thought you might like at the store. And Mrs. Pierce had some fresh oatmeal cookies baked. I brought you a batch."

"Well, thank you, boss," Cameron said. She gave him the knife, which was sheathed. It was bone handled, with a six-inch blade, double-edged, slightly curved, fitted with a blood groove. "Very nice," he said, fitting it on his belt.

"I hoped you'd like it." Cassie looked around the ranch. "Did you get some rest yesterday?"

"Some," he replied. Before he could say anything else, Cassie, looking toward the creek, said:

"Cameron! What did I tell you?"

"What do you mean?"

"The cattle . . . there must be a dozen head that weren't here yesterday."

"That's not important right now," he said, waving a hand. "Look, we have to talk, Cassie. I'll put your horse up. Why don't you go into the house and rinse off. I'll be along."

. She gave him a curious look, but agreed and walked off

66

toward the house as Cameron swung the saddle from the bay's back and rubbed it down before letting it into the corral to join the other horses.

He walked to the house himself, pausing to rinse off himself at the outside pump.

Cassie was at the table when he went in. Coffee was boiling on the wood stove.

Her eyes watched him expectantly. Obviously something was wrong.

"What is it, Cameron?"

"We had an Apache raid last night."

"Oh, no!" she said with dismay. "I didn't notice anything missing or damaged. Did they get away with any of the horses?"

"Only the black one," he said, and her eyes leaped with surprise before she got herself under control once again. She tried to speak calmly, but Cameron could hear emotion in her shaky voice.

"What black horse?"

"The one with the white stocking and white star," Cameron said quietly.

Cassie rose and went to the stove where the coffee was burbling. She kept her back to him as she poured them each a cup.

"I'm afraid I don't know what you mean, Cameron. I haven't any such horse."

"Who does?"

"I'm sure I don't know," she said. She wore a thin mock smile as she returned to the table bearing the two coffee cups.

"Are you sure?"

"Yes," she said emphatically. She was lying, Cameron was sure, but he didn't press it. She stared into her coffee cup for a long time and then lifted her eyes.

"How did this black horse come to be here?" she asked. "Did you see who rode it in?"

"No, I was up in the hills trying to find a few strays to bring in. When I got back—there it was, the bit slipped, hitched to your rail. I poked around but there was no one here at all."

"How strange," she said, but there seemed to be relief in her voice on hearing that Cameron Black had not seen the rider of the horse.

"Very strange," Cameron agreed. Well, if she didn't want to tell him, that was her business. He had something else on his mind as well.

"Maybe," he said, "you ought to reconsider staying in town until we know for sure this band of Apaches has cleared out of the area. You never know when they might be back and if they catch us unaware, the two of us won't be much of a match for them. I was lucky last night, just lucky."

"No!" Her eyes and voice were defiant. "I won't be driven off. We'll just have to take extra precautions, that's all, Cameron."

"Just a thought. I don't want you to get hurt, that's all," Cameron Black said.

"I'd rather stay and fight for what's mine," she said positively. "Even so"—she paused before continuing—"I might consider it if you could go with me. I wouldn't feel right about leaving you here alone. But," she said with a sigh, "you can't go into Fortune—ever."

"What do you mean?"

"There were some men—five of them—in Fortune yesterday. They were asking about a tall man who rode a gray horse." She hesitated. "They had your name,

Cameron, and they put up a reward for you. A thousand dollars."

"My horse?"

"They haven't found it yet, but you know they will. The single flaw in my plan is that they might think you're holed up in Fortune, that your horse went lame or simply was worn to the nub and that you hiked back to Fortune."

"The kid . . ."

"I talked to Jake. Believe me, he won't say a word," Cassie assured him. "So you see, we're sort of stuck out here, aren't we?"

"I guess we are," Cameron agreed, taking a deep drink of his coffee. Then more brightly: "Why don't you break out those oatmeal cookies. Let's see what kind of baker old Mrs. Pierce is."

"All right," Cassie agreed. "Let's indulge ourselves. What are you going to do the rest of the day?"

"I brought in a calf yesterday. If you'll tell me where your branding iron is, I'll slap a brand on it before I do anything." Cassie was back with a plate full of cookies. Cameron took one and asked, "By the way, speaking of brands, have you ever seen a horse wearing a Rocking K brand?"

"Rocking K?" Her voice again was shaky. "Why, no. And if there was such a brand around here, I'm sure I would have seen it."

Then she drifted off onto other subjects and Cameron, munching Mrs. Pierce's oatmeal and molasses cookies, could only listen, watch, and wonder.

Nine

Cameron built a small branding fire and walked to the barn to get the old S+S iron. He took a lariat and on foot stalked and roped the calf, then carried it back to the fire, where he threw it and hog-tied it. The iron was already plenty hot and he touched it to the calf's hide, smelling the burning hair and skin as the calf bawled. Then he untied it and watched as the frightened youngster beelined it back toward the safety of its mother.

Cameron kicked out the fire and replaced the branding iron in the barn. Then he stood in the barn door for a while looking toward the hills. There was a temptation to return to them and see how many more strays he could round up—but that would mean leaving Cassie alone. No, he would work around the ranch today—keeping his rifle always nearby.

One section of the barn roof was in bad shape and he discussed repairing it with Cassie. She seemed distracted most of the day and now she just waved a hand limply.

"If you want to, Cameron. It's one thing Dad was going to do. There's tar paper and shingles he bought in that storage shed behind the barn. I'm not sure where the ladder got to."

"I'll find it. Cassie, are you feeling all right?" he asked.

"Yes, why?"

"Just wondered. You look a little pale, tired."

"I'm fine. Don't worry about me. I've got a little cleaning up to do. Go on and do your job."

"I'd feel better if you took your own advice and rested up until you're a hundred percent," Black said.

"I *am* a hundred percent," she said with a laugh, teasingly pushing him toward the door. "You just want me to fall asleep so I won't know when you're dogging it."

He paused still, studying her, and she ordered: "Get going now!"

"Yes, boss," he answered, touching the brim of his hat. Then he went out into the heat of the desert day and got to work.

Propping the old ladder up at the rear of the barn, he carried the roll of tar paper and bale of shingle up onto the roof. Returning for hammer and nails he paused long enough to fashion a sling from some twine he found in the shed. With the rifle on his back then he clambered up once more to begin ripping the old, decayed shingles from the roof.

His eyes went constantly to the hills as he worked. The sun beat down incessantly, burning his back and exposed neck. He tied his bandanna differently, covering the maximum of skin, and worked on.

Now and then Cassie Shore would emerge from the house. Sometimes she would wave at him, at other times she too would simply gaze. But she did not look toward the hills where the Apaches lurked, but toward town.

Yes, she had her secrets and her problems, but

71

Cameron could do nothing to help her unless he knew what they were.

What about the men hunting him? he wondered. Had they drifted out of Fortune or not? Maybe they had left a man behind. Maybe they didn't have to. With a reward out for Cameron Black, the townspeople would do their work for them.

If not for Cassie, he would have moved on; but there was no way he could leave her under these circumstances. He could only hope for the best.

For both of them.

The roof took longer than he had expected. By dusk he still wasn't finished with the laborious work. He climbed back down and stood mopping his face with his bandanna as the shadows pooled at the base of the craggy bluff.

A horse nickered in the corral and Black smiled.

"All right, rag head. I know what you want."

Cameron Black walked behind the house to the apple tree and plucked four apples from it. Returning to the corral, he gave them to the horses, stroking the buckskin's neck as he fed it. The horse nudged him with his nose and Cameron said, "No more tonight. Come morning, all right?"

He cleaned up outside and went on into the house. Cassie had made a stew out of the leftover beef and the scent of it was steamy, tempting. His own clothes, washed now, were folded on the sofa.

"Thanks for doing the laundry, Cassie," he called. "I'm going to change now. Better stay out there."

"Go ahead, but don't be long," she called.

Dinner was eaten in near silence that evening. The only light note was struck when Cassie commented: "You're never going to get that apple pie if you keep giving the apples to the horses."

"No, and now I've got them expecting it." Briefly he explained how that had started, with him trying to calm and befriend the buckskin.

"You've been riding Captain Jack?" she asked in surprise.

"Is that his name? Yes. He's the one I used to bring the cattle in. He's worked cattle before."

"Yes." Her voice was subdued. "He was Dad's horse. His cutting horse. No one's ridden him since . . ."

"If you don't want me to ride it, I won't," Cameron Black said.

"No, no. That's all right," she replied, but then she fell into silence again.

After supper they sat in the living room, Cassie on the sofa, Cameron on the stuffed chair in the corner. She had broken out her needlepoint, which she worked on with deep concentration while Cameron cleaned his weapons for a while. He found some gun oil in the pantry and he worked over the action on revolver and rifle.

That completed, he built a fire. It wasn't cold, but this was a very small fire, a looking fire. The kind useful for thinking.

He watched the curlicues and spirals, the darting tongues of red and gold flame, the occasional spark as the fire touched pitch, and he fell into meditation, nearly hypnotized by the softly burning flames.

He was leaning forward, his chin resting on folded hands, moving not at all except to blink. The flames were touching a deep part of him, one he had tried to smother.

"What are you thinking?" Cassie asked.

He started as if she had awakened him from a deep sleep. She had put her needlepoint work aside and was

73

watching him with dark, firelit eyes.

"Nothing at all."

"Cameron?"

"I don't like to talk about it."

"It might help."

"Nothing helps," he said. "You can't raise the dead."

"Who was she?" Cassie asked.

He shook his head and leaned back in his chair. Cassie thought he was not going to answer, but eventually he did, speaking in a monotone.

"Susan McCulloch. We were supposed to be married. Our families had neighboring ranches down Texas way. Near Nacogdoches.

"We were just kids, really, but we were determined. She and I seemed meant for each other. We grew up together." Black was silent for a minute. He rose and poked at the low fire, bringing it back to life.

"She just had her ma and pa and a Mexican hand to work the spread so me and my brother, Simon, would go over and help at roundup time and such.

"Her folks were all for the wedding as soon as I had finished building the house Simon and me were building. My pa—he was all for it too. Susan used to come visiting and bring him pies and such. Dad was crippled up from a fall off his horse some years back when we had a stampede during one of those damned thunder and lightning summer storms. He would surely brighten up when Susan came visiting."

Black again was silent. Cassie watched him, seeing the faraway look in his eyes, the tension in the muscles of his neck.

"What happened?" she asked.

It took him a long time to go on. Finally he looked at

her again and said, "One winter night I went out to fetch some wood. There was patchy snow on the ground . . . I saw smoke from the McCulloch spread . . . dropped the wood and got my horse. I never bothered to saddle him. Slipped him the bit, heeled him, and lit out. When I reached the house it was engulfed in flames.

"I kicked in the kitchen door and was hit by a wall of heat and smoke. Circling I went to the parlor and smashed in the window.

"Susan was there on the floor. I got her out the window, but I knew it was no good. Her body was cold. There was something sticky on her chest: blood. She'd been shot.

"I moved like a man asleep back toward the window. I knew Mr. and Mrs. McCulloch slept upstairs and thought I could get to them, but it was already too late. The entire house was an inferno. Timbers started to drop, and there were flames shooting out of all the doors and windows upstairs.

"I picked Susan up, hoping still somehow, though I already knew, and I carried her back under the chestnut tree.

"Then I saw the man who had done it. He came around the corner of the house on his horse, spurring it like the devil. He was just a shadow against the glow of the flames. I fired five shots at him and then kept firing on the spent chambers. Then I just sat there with Susan."

"Do you know who it was?"

"No. My first thought was that it was Garcia, the Mexican hand. He was the only other one around, but he came stumbling up to me on foot, hatless, barefoot, his face smudged with smoke.

"What did you do then?" Susan asked.

75

"What was there to do? I sat there until dawn, until the fire burned out, and then I buried Susan beneath the chestnut tree. Then I started wandering. I couldn't stay there anymore. I grabbed my rifle, saddled my bay, and said good-bye."

Cassie was silent, watching the fire as it burned low. Black went on.

"Tried my hand as a blacksmith—wasn't much good at that," he admitted with a crooked smile. "Worked cattle for a few outfits. Joined the army. Tried to run a freight operation. Was a lawman for three days." He smiled again at some secret reminiscence.

Cassie Shore said softly. "I'm sorry, Cameron."

"It's been a long time," he answered.

"Time doesn't always erase pain."

"No, but you learn you can't do a thing to change the past. It's best to work on the problems of the present."

There was a veiled hint there, but Cassie refused to rise to the bait. Her own secret was too near for her to speak of. If Black had opened up to her, he knew it would be a while yet before the woman told him her own problems.

"I was thinking . . ." Cassie began, but Cameron held up a hand for silence. He listened intently and heard it again: a horse nickering—but it didn't come from the corral, but from across the creek.

He crossed the room, Cassie's frightened eyes on him. He blew out the lamp and handed her the Winchester.

"What is it?"

"Stay here, pull the latchstring, and don't let it out for anyone but me."

Then Black tugged off his boots, moved to the window, and slipped out into the night, revolver in hand.

76

Ten

Cameron Black crouched in the shadows beside the house, his eyes darting from point to point. The moon was rising now and the shadows before every tree and rock seemed to be shifting, living things. The creek itself writhed southward, moving sinuously. He saw nothing, heard nothing.

And then the horse nickered again. It was a distant sound, but unmistakable. Cameron, barefoot, started toward the creek. Crossing it, he hung in the shade of the big cottonwood there and waited, his thumb slowly drawing back the hammer of the Remington .44.

There was movement to his left then—a man moving forward in a crouch, a step at a time. He was no more than fifty feet away and moving nearer.

Cameron let him draw within another twenty feet. He was ready then to step out and challenge the man, to fire if necessary, for the prowler was carrying a long gun in his hands—that much was obvious by moonlight.

He had started to take that first step out from behind the tree when he heard gravel crunch off to his right.

Damn all, there were two of them.

Making a quick decision, Cameron holstered his pistol and drew the knife Cassie had given him from its sheath. He pressed his back to the cottonwood and waited, his heart thumping.

He saw the muzzle of a rifle and the brim of a hat, and the creeping man passed the tree, eyes fixed on the ranch house. Cameron let him take one more step and then swiftly and as deadly as a big cat he moved behind the man, one hand going under his chin, exposing the throat, locking his mouth shut as the knife did its bloody work, ripping across the stalking man's throat, honed steel slashing deep.

He slumped in Cameron's grip and Cameron Black lowered him silently to the ground. Cameron bent, picked up the man's rifle and his hat, which he put on. Then he started creeping back toward the yard, moving in the same crouching, shuffling gait the prowler had used.

He thought he saw and then definitely saw the second man now, moving slowly toward the creek. He couldn't identify any features and knew the other man couldn't tell that it was a stranger who now stalked the ranch house with him. The moon was at their backs, their faces deep in shadow. Cameron, wearing the other man's hat and moving in the same way, would appear to be one and the same. There had been no shots, nothing to alarm the second outlaw.

Cameron moved nearer to the other man. They crossed the creek almost together, thirty paces apart. As they emerged from the rill, Cameron Black moved still nearer. He wanted to surprise this one, get the drop on him and get some answers.

Was it him they wanted? Was it Cassie? Were they

simply roving raiders?

The other man angrily jabbed a finger toward the far side of the house, obviously wanting Cameron Black to flank it. Black acted as if he hadn't seen it and moved nearer yet.

Suddenly something—perhaps the stranger had noticed Cameron's lack of boots—alerted the stalker.

"What the hell!" he shouted, and he spun toward Cameron, bringing his rifle to his shoulder. Cameron didn't waste the motion. He fired from the hip, twice. The stalker was flung back to lie on his back against the hard-packed earth of the yard. Cameron rushed to him.

His shots had been all too good. The man wouldn't be able to tell him anything. He wouldn't be able to tell anyone anything ever again.

The night was vastly still and quiet except for the frightened whickering of one of the horses and the bawling of a steer.

Cameron searched the man's pockets but found only a twenty-dollar gold piece and a silver pocket watch. Standing, he sighed and walked back toward the house.

He rapped on the door and shouted, "It's me, Cassie! Open up."

He heard her light footsteps cross the floor and as she opened the door saw the fear in her eyes.

"I heard shots. You're all right?" she said it almost in wonder.

"All right."

She threw her arms around him and clung to him for a long minute, and when she drew back there were tears in her eyes. "What was it?" she asked.

"That's what I want to ask you. Light the lantern, will you?" By what remained of the fire's glow he tugged his

79

boots on. When Cassie gave him the lantern he rose and said, "Come on. I want to see if you know these men."

"I don't . . ." her voice was trembling.

"I know you don't want to see them," he snapped, "but it might be important."

The moon had escaped the horizon fully now and rode high and graceful, a paling, brilliant globe against the clear desert sky. Along the ridge the pinyon pines stood like a rank of dark warriors.

Cameron Black led the woman to where the man he had shot lay and held the lantern over the man's face. His eyes were goggled out, his face tight with shock in death.

Cameron was sure that he hadn't seen the man before. He looked questioningly at Cassie.

"Well?"

"No," she said, but there was a hesitation in her voice. Cameron's mouth tightened, but he said nothing.

"Come on—hoist your skirt," he said, and he led her across the creek to where the other man lay.

She gasped as she saw the blood the knife had spilled—quarts of it—and the slash across his throat. Cameron put the lantern down and as he searched this man's pockets he asked her again if she had seen him before.

"No, not him either," she said. Again Cameron didn't believe her.

"All right," he said with a sharp exhalation. "Let's go."

She started to turn back toward the ranch house, but Cameron held her by the arm, stopping her. "Not that way," he said, "upslope."

"But why . . .?"

He had already started on and now she scurried after him. Cameron stopped from time to time, listening, and finally he heard it.

"This way," he said, and she followed obediently.

Tethered to the scrub oak was a paint pony which shifted its feet nervously as Cameron approached.

Standing next to it was a black horse with a white stocking and a white star on its forehead.

It looked trail weary; it carried saddlebags behind the saddle. Cameron untied both horses and started back toward the ranch.

"You should leave them here . . . turn them loose," Cassie said, and from the tone of her voice it was clear now that she did know something about the black horse. Cameron Black was fed up with her secretiveness, and after unsaddling the two horses and turning them into the corral he returned to the house determined to find out just what was going on.

She had laid a few twigs on the fire and sat now staring at it. As he entered she looked up, knowledge of what was to come in her eyes.

"All right, Cassie, let's have it."

"I don't know what you mean," she stammered.

He crouched down in front of her, the fire crackling in the stone fireplace at his back.

"Listen, lady, I could have gotten myself killed out there tonight. I had to kill two men to protect you. I think I deserve an explanation. Who are they and why are they out to get you?"

"It's not me they want," she blurted, "it's you, Cameron."

"Me?" He snorted. "I've never seen them before. Do you mean they somehow found out where I was, that they wanted the reward?"

"They couldn't collect a reward."

"You're talking in circles," Cameron said, rising in frustration.

"They're outlaws!" she shouted. "They'd be shot on sight in Fortune."

He had broken the ice anyway, gotten her tongue to loosen up a bit. Now he waited for her to go further with what she knew. With a heavy sigh she leaned back against the back of the sofa. Finally her eyes met his and she said:

"I knew them both. Randy Fann and Jake Snow. The horse belongs to Abel Packett. They must have been expecting him, so they left his horse here.

"They must have been camped in the hills waiting for Abel. The last I heard he was in prison, but he must be out by now or they wouldn't have left his horse. When they saw you they retrieved the horse, not knowing who you were, maybe thinking you'd recognize the horse. They wouldn't want anyone around when Abel got here.

"When they saw you were here to stay they must have decided you had to go. I shouldn't have brought you out here . . . I just thought, hoped it was all over."

Cameron's brow furrowed. "What was all over, Cassie? What have these men got to do with you?"

"Don't you understand? My father . . . we needed money badly one year. He agreed to let some men stay out here, knowing they were outlaws. Abel Packett paid well. They'd ride out, sometimes for weeks, but they always came back. They'd discovered a good hideout and were determined not to give it up.

"My father pled with them, but they just laughed in his face. He had only intended to put them up that first time to make a little extra money, but now he couldn't get rid of them. He couldn't go to the law himself. He was implicated too.

"Each time they rode out we prayed they wouldn't come back, but they always did. Until Abel Packett got shot and then arrested trying to rob a freight office down at Tyler.

"After he got locked up the gang separated and drifted away."

"When was this?" Cameron asked.

"Only a year or so ago. I can't believe they let him out this soon. He must have escaped."

"Your father died about a year ago. Are you sure it was the Apaches that got him?"

"If you'd seen the body . . . yes, I'm sure. There's an irony to it all. The Apaches must have been aware that there were half a dozen men with guns down here most of the time. They stayed away as long as Abel Packett's mob was here."

For a moment she was lost in dark thoughtfulness, then she said quietly, "You have to go, Cameron."

"Do you want me to?"

"No! But you have to, don't you see. They had set up a rendezvous. Something must have delayed Abel Packett. When he arrives he'll kill you. You killed two of his men tonight!"

"I'll ask you again—do you want me to go?"

"Cameron, I want nothing more in the world than for you to stay." Her eyes were misted as she spoke. The fire popped once.

"Then I'll stay. We'll figure something out."

"*What?* What can you hope to do against them?" Cassie wagged her head heavily. "We can't ask for any help in Fortune. I'd have to admit what my father did; they'd find out you were here."

"Another sheltered outlaw," Cameron said with a

83

faint smile.

"That's not funny, Cameron."

"No," he said thoughtfully, "it's not." His eyes grew serious.

"What are you thinking?" she asked.

"Just that that might be the way to handle this. Look, Cassie, Packett and his mob haven't been around for a long time. You needed some money. I'm an outlaw on the run. You decided to let me hide out here if I could pay. After all, that's how your father made his extra money.

"Packett is going to be short of men now. He might just need an extra gunman. Me."

"Cameron, you can't get in that deep," she said. Her astonished expression widened her dark eyes and caused her mouth to open.

"I can't think of another way except getting you out of here, and you won't leave. I won't leave you alone with a gang of outlaws. It'll work, Cassie. We have to do a few things first. You were right about the horses. I'll lead them up into the sandhills and turn them loose. The Apaches will snatch them up in no time. I'll bury the bodies and the tack as well.

"Can you get hold of a poster on me in Fortune?"

"Yes," she said shakily. "There's three or four tacked up around town."

"Okay. You ride in tomorrow and bring one back. My credentials, you might say," he said humorlessly.

"Cameron—do you know what you're doing?"

"I wouldn't go that far," Cameron Black said with a hint of a smile on his broad mouth, "but I haven't got a better plan, do you?"

"Cameron, if Packett even suspects . . ."

"I know, Cassie." He walked to her and cupped her

face in his hands. Looking down at her worried eyes he felt an emotion which had long been absent. He bent his face to hers and kissed her on the lips. Then he turned and started toward the door.

"Where are you going, Cameron?"

"To find a shovel. It's going to be a long night."

Eleven

Each outlaw was thrown over a horse. Cameron saddled the buckskin and led his morbid caravan where the digging would be easier. The moon shone eerily on the dunes, making deep moon shadows in the hollows. Distantly a coyote howled—that same coyote. The one that wore war paint.

Cameron couldn't do this job too close to the house, nor could he venture too far into the Apaches' domain. He turned eastward, heeling the buckskin up into the farther sandhills. No one would have any reason to come this way.

The buckskin went to its knees in sand sometimes, but they finally topped a ridge and on a dune-swept mesa Cameron Black swung down and began his grisly chore.

By moonlight he dug the two graves and rolled the outlaws into them. Then he dug a pit for their saddles and gear. He was bathed in sweat although the night was cool. The moon had rolled over toward the western horizon before he was finished.

The horses were still standing there when he was

finally done. They couldn't be allowed to follow him back to the ranch. With a branch broken from a dead sagebrush he walked toward them, waving his hands, whipping them across the haunches, driving them away, deeper into the hills where the Apaches would undoubtedly find them in the morning.

The buckskin was watching him with wary eyes and Black laughed, tossing the stick away.

"No, not you, Captain Jack," Cameron said. He swung aboard and walked the buckskin back out of the sandhills toward the valley below, looking over his shoulder now and then to make sure the horses weren't following . . . or the Apaches.

Cassie had fallen asleep on the couch. The fire had long since gone to embers and then died out. Cameron Black settled into the chair, crossed his arms, and fell off into a dreamless sleep himself.

In the morning, after a breakfast of biscuits and gravy, followed by coffee, Cassie headed off toward town. Cameron had given her the gold piece he had found on the outlaw in case she needed some supplies. He himself got to work finishing the barn roof.

Neither of them, by tacit agreement, had spoken of the night before, but the memory of it hung heavy in the air around them.

Cameron worked swiftly, but automatically. There was too much to think about, too much that was deeply troublesome: the Indians up in the hills, the outlaws, his own pursuers.

And Cassie.

His feelings for her were growing too strong too soon. He had gotten himself backed into a corner. Logic told him to saddle the buckskin and get the hell out of there, ride for California or back to Texas. But logic took no notice of those needful, deep brown eyes of Cassie Shore.

After Susan he had thought he would never find another woman. He had had a few flings, but they hadn't meant much. Susan was always there in the back of his mind, preventing any deeper attachment. This was different, very different. And no matter what logic wanted, Cameron Black was going to stick it out. He had given his word.

And there was no place he wanted to go without Cassie Shore.

Even if he could have convinced her to leave her ranch, which she obviously loved so dearly, what could he offer her? A life on the run without any defined prospects? She deserved better, much better.

He shook his thoughts clear, forcing himself to concentrate on the roofing. Still he looked constantly toward town, awaiting her return.

"Are you sure that's his horse?" the Mexican asked. He was picking his teeth with a penknife as his boss ran a hand across the flank of the gray horse.

"Of course I'm sure, damn it. Don't you think I've seen this horse before. It's Cameron Black's. Look at the brand, you dumb greaser."

The Mexican flinched at the word "greaser," but he went on smiling and looked at the Texas brand. The Rafter B was blurred but still easily read on the big gray's flank.

His boss, the lanky man with the black eyes and narrow mustache, was rigid with emotion. His eyes were a study in intensity. He ran a finger over the brand again and again. Then he crouched and with knowledgeable hands again tested each quarter for infirmity. He found none.

"It's not lame. The shoes are tight. Why did he turn it loose?" the leader of the band of men asked no one in particular. Around him half a dozen men stood or squatted, watching the black-eyed man.

They were a tough band of men, but none of them would have liked to cross their boss. Simply, he was mad and they all knew it. It took little to trigger him. But he paid well, very well, and so long as you kept your mouth shut, things were okay. It beat punching cattle.

He was obsessed with this Cameron Black, that was all they knew. They had been trailing him for over a month now after the botched attempt at killing him down south.

"Why did he leave the horse?" The black-eyed man rose and turned toward his gang. "You idiots should have had him a long time ago. Why do I have to do everything myself?"

Again no one spoke. They were used to his flare-ups, to his rages. The Mexican, whose name was Dominguez, had heard him the night before cursing and raging in his sleep at Black. Now the black-eyed man turned coldly logical.

"The horse wasn't lame. He only had the one horse. We know that from tracking him. He couldn't hope to escape on foot."

"Maybe," the redhead named Forrest suggested, "the gray was just worn out and Cameron Black bought a fresh horse from somebody passing by or at some ranch close by."

The black-eyed man paid no attention to the suggestion. He looked toward the far mesa topped with a hint of green, a few tilted, wind-stunted trees, as if he expected to see Cameron Black there.

"He's here," the gang leader said. "He's nearby, I can feel it."

"You want to search the town?" the big man, Cummings, asked.

"I want to search it, yes. The posters might not do any good. If he's paying someone they might not turn him in. The town . . . not storming through it, but casually. He can't stay hidden forever. Then we'll see if there's any outlying ranches where he could have gone. Find out if anyone might have sold him a fresh horse."

He turned to the Indian, Campo, and said, "Go on up the trail, Campo, and see if you can pick up a trail that might be Cameron Black's. Wally, you go with him," he instructed the walrus-mustached gang member. "If you run across him, no one man is going to take him. I know Cameron Black."

The Indian snorted derisively. He had never yet met the man he could not take on his own. But he said nothing. The gold he was earning meant even more than his pride.

The two scouts rode out ahead, leaving Rattlesnake Canyon behind. The others waited for their boss to remount and, leading the gray horse by a hastily fashioned hackamore, returned to Fortune to see what could be discovered.

The black-eyed man scowled as he rode. His body was rigid still. These idiots had botched the job. How could Cameron Black have escaped? He should have taken charge of the job himself. But he hadn't wanted Cameron Black to see him. He would have recognized him in an instant.

That night . . . Black had seen him.

90

He remembered the struggle with Susan McCulloch, the old man trying to stop him as he ripped at Susan's dress. He had to shoot the old man and then his wife.

It wasn't his fault—the bitch had wanted him. He could tell by her teasing eyes. But she always pretended she wanted Cameron Black.

That was the way these bitches were. She didn't have the strength to stop him from getting what he had come for. When he was done she just lay there sobbing, and he realized that she would tell everyone who had done the killing. There was nothing to do but kill her too.

Then he had set the fire to cover the crime.

The fire too had fascinated him, and he had dawdled too long watching as the house went up in curling, spouting crimson flame.

Then that damned Cameron Black had arrived and dragged the girl's body out of the house.

The black-eyed man had whipped his horse out of there, but Cameron Black saw him. He emptied his pistol at him. Tagged the horse the black-eyed man rode. Then both of them started drifting.

It was a long chance they would ever meet again in the vastness of the West, but one day Black was there, in the very town the black-eyed man had chosen to set up his latest venture, the saloon.

And those stupid fools had tried to cheat him, then had let Cameron Black get away. There was no choice now but to find Cameron Black and kill him before the black-eyed man was hung.

Find him he would. Find him and kill him personally.

In a way he had qualms about it . . . their roots were intertwined. But it was kill or be killed, wasn't it? And

Simon Black would rather have it be his brother than himself.

Abel Packett skirted the town widely. He rode alone. The rest of the gang would meet him at the old hideout within a few days. Snow and Fann should already be there.

Packett whipped the stumpy bay horse he was riding. The horse wasn't worth a damn. It would feel good to have Excalibur, the big black, under him again. That horse could easily outdistance any pony a lawman could afford.

Once he had that horse back and had his gang together again, somebody was going to pay for that year in Yuma Territorial Prison.

He thought of the hideout again, wondering if that nice little piece of fluff, what was her name—Cassie?—was still living there. She would be unless some clodhopping kid had married her and taken her off somewhere.

After a year in prison, thoughts of her were more than merely stimulating.

Abel Packett had plans, many plans—and no one was going to stand in his way. He was going to make this territory stand up and take notice.

His eyes narrowed suddenly. He peered through the heat haze toward the town of Fortune. A woman on a bay horse was riding west, toward the old hideout. It could only be one woman and Abel Packett whipped his weary mount into motion; he wanted to catch up with Cassie Shore.

Distance and the weary horse were against his plan. It wasn't until they were nearly into the yard of the Shore ranch that Abel Packett caught up.

Cassie's head turned and her eyes flashed with fear and surprise.

"Hello, Cassie," Packett said, his lopsided grin evil and mocking.

She was surprised enough by his sudden appearance that her stuttering welcome was realistic.

"Abel! I thought you were . . . what a surprise to see you here."

"A surprise?" His eyes sharpened beneath the brim of his hat. "What about Snow and Fann? They were supposed to be here and tell you I was coming."

"No," she said, her voice regaining a steadiness which surprised her, "they haven't been around. Not unless they rode in today while I was in town."

"Damn them . . ." Then he spotted the man on the barn roof. "Who's that, then?" he demanded.

"A hand I took on. Dad died, you know. The Apaches. I can't handle this place alone."

"Get rid of him," Abel Packett snapped.

"I can't," Cassie protested. "I took his money."

"You get paid by hired hands now?" Abel Packett asked. His hand reached out, took Cassie's horse's bridle, and halted her horse beside his own. "All right, what is this?"

"The same as it was with you, Abel. After Dad died things got real rough out here. I only knew one way to make some quick money."

From her skirt pocket she took the folded wanted poster of Cameron Black. "He's all right, Abel."

Abel Packett studied the poster for a long time, his eyes lifting once to the roof of the barn. He handed the poster back to Cassie.

"We'll see," was all he said, and although Cassie's

heart seemed to miss one beat, her nerves were slightly calmer. Abel Packett was muttering to himself. Aloud, he said:

"I wonder where those fools got off to. They didn't even leave Excalibur?"

"No, Abel. I haven't seen hide nor hair of anyone or your horse."

Together now they walked their horses into the yard. Cameron Black, spotted them, climbed back down the ladder, and, wiping his forehead, stepped forward to meet them.

Abel halted his horse and studied the tall man who was approaching them. He liked the way he moved, the way he wore his gun; but he was habitually suspicious— that had kept him alive this long.

"You're Cameron Black?" he demanded.

"That's right."

"Where you from, Black."

"Texas, mostly," Cameron answered.

"We'll talk later. Cool my horse off and put him up," Packett ordered.

Black had decided to play the game. He had to let this man play top dog, yet he couldn't seem to have no backbone himself and be pushed around—not if he was to represent himself as a hard-bitten outlaw.

"Put it up yourself," Cameron answered, his hand near his gun.

Cassie had caught onto the game quickly. "Cameron— this is Abel Packett."

"Packett?" Cameron said with what he hoped was suitable awe. He peered curiously at the newcomer. "Heard of you."

"You'll hear more. Put my horse up, why don't you,"

Packett asked. His ego had been preened by Cameron's apparent respect for his name.

Still Cameron held his ground grudgingly for a moment. He didn't want to appear to give in too easily. Finally he agreed, "Sure, Mr. Packett. I'll take care of him for you. Only thing—I ain't normally a stable hand."

"I didn't think you were," Packett said. Then, a smug expression on his face, he swung down and walked stiffly toward the water pump. It had been a long ride and he was hot and dry.

"Cameron," Cassie whispered, "don't take it too far."

"Don't worry. Not yet."

No, for now he would play Abel Packett's game. What he would have liked to have done was show Mr. Packett the sandhills, but that would be just too dangerous for Cassie when the rest of the gang arrived. For now he would play lackey.

The time to take care of Mr. Packett would come.

Twelve

Packett waited impatiently the next few days. He grew angrier and angrier. "Where the hell are Snow and Fann?" he demanded of no one in particular. He and Cameron Black were at the corral, aimlessly watching the horses.

"Apaches," Cameron said.

"What?" Packett's head snapped around, eyes blazing.

"Maybe Apaches got 'em. The Indians've been lurking around the ranch. Maybe they've been scalped and baked by now."

Packett cursed softly. The notion was all too possible. The truth was that he was more concerned about his horse than his two lieutenants. The thought of some naked savage mounted on Excalibur was enough to raise his blood pressure a few notches.

"What kind of work do you do?" Packett asked, and Cameron Black knew what he meant.

"Whatever I can pick up. Anything but powder."

"I've got a powder man, but I don't like that much.

96

Saw the whole roof of a bank in San Antonio go up once. Don't like powder, don't like trains."

"Trains are tough," Cameron Black agreed.

Packett looked Black up and down. "How'd you find this place, Black?"

"I sort of got pushed to it," Cameron said in response. "There were a few people chasing me out on the desert. I just stumbled across Fortune and the woman stumbled across me."

"You're sleeping in the house."

"On the couch, yeah."

"That ain't much of a bed in the back of that buckboard," Packett said suggestively. Cameron knew what he was coming around to. It was obvious the way the outlaw's eyes followed Cassie.

"No. The couch ain't much either."

"Look, Black, I mean to sleep in the house on that couch," Packett said through clenched teeth. "Understand me?"

"All right," Cameron said, nodding amiably. "You can have it"—Packett's cruel eyes were glittering—"as soon as I move into the bedroom, how's that?"

Packett's face became masklike. "What do you mean?" he asked tightly.

"Didn't Cassie tell you?" Cameron Black asked, tilting his hat back. "We're going to get married."

Without another word Abel Packett turned on his heel and stalked away in the direction of the creek, leaving a grinning Cameron Black to watch his back.

At dinner he told Cassie, "I didn't know what else to tell him. He has a lot of ideas about you, Cassie. You'll just have to keep up the pretense."

"It's all right," she said, but her voice was strangely

97

quiet. She cleaned the table off and began washing dishes even before Cameron had finished his coffee and dessert. He shrugged mentally. He never would understand women.

That was the evening two more outlaws rode in. Abel Packett emerged hatless from the barn to watch their arrival and Cameron Black, Cassie beside him, stepped out onto the porch as well.

"The one with the beard—that's Dan Beeman. He's killed half a dozen men. Usually with a knife." She gripped Cameron Black's arm, shuddering.

"And the other one?" Cameron asked, indicating the whip-lean kid whose blond hair tumbled out everywhere from beneath his broad-brimmed hat.

"He was only here once. They just called him Kid. I don't know anything about him, but if he rides with Abel Packett, you know he's dirty."

"I guess I'd better introduce myself," Cameron Black said. Abel Packett was shaking hands with the Kid, laughing at something Beeman said. Cassie gripped Cameron's arm but he patted her hand and smiled. "It'll be all right. I'm in too deep to do anything else now."

Cameron crossed the hard-packed yard in long strides. The newcomers eyed him with suspicion and Abel Packett with a sort of superior humor as if the arrival of more muscle and guns proved beyond a doubt who was in charge here.

"Hello, boys," Black said easily, sticking out his hand, "I'm Cameron Black."

Neither of the two outlaws took the extended hand. Packett said, "It's all right—Cameron's in with us."

That was news to Cameron Black, but it led to instant acceptance. The two new arrivals now shook hands with

98

him and introduced themselves.

It was Beeman, the big black-bearded man who asked, "Where's Snow and Fann?"

"They never showed up," Packett said dryly. "Black thinks maybe the Apaches got 'em. I think maybe he's right."

"How long are we going to have to wait for them?" the Kid asked.

"We're not waiting," Packett said. "I've got something in mind the four of us can handle just fine. To hell with Snow and Fann. Either they're dead or it's just plain their tough luck. It's time for a payday, boys." He turned toward Cameron. "Can you handle a stagecoach job?"

"I can handle anything if the pay's right," Black answered casually.

"Where?" Dan Beeman asked.

"On the Butterfield Trail. This side of Boron where they have to make that long grade. They usually have a shotgun rider, that's all."

"Passengers?" the Kid asked. "I saw old Bill Chase get his head blown off looking inside the coach."

"They don't usually carry 'em—just don't look inside," Packett said, drawing an appreciative chuckle from Beeman.

"How do we get over and back?" Cameron Black asked.

Packett looked at him as if he had no right to ask any questions.

"Out past Fortune. In over the hills." He nodded toward the hills beyond the ranch.

"Past the Apaches?" Black said in genuine surprise.

"They won't fool with four armed men," Packett said confidently. The Kid and Beeman exchanged a dubious glance, but said nothing. What Abel Packett said went

99

with them.

"When?" the Kid asked.

"Morning. Clean your weapons, see to your horses, bed down early. We'll be riding at sunrise." He turned to Cameron Black and with some animosity said, "Get your woman to fix us some vittles."

Cameron stood in the kitchen, leaning against the wall beside the spice rack, arms folded. He had just finished telling Cassie what was about to happen. She just gawked at him.

"And you're going with them! You're going to help them do this!"

"No choice, Cassie. What happens if I refuse."

"You're going to stick up a stage! I can't believe it."

"If I don't go both you and I are in deep trouble," Black told her. "Besides, if I go I may have a chance to prevent some violence, may have a chance to foul up the job. I can't do either here."

"I don't like it, Cameron, I don't like it at all," she said, shaking her head in protest.

"I don't like it either, Cassie. You must know that."

Cassie didn't respond. "We ought to get out of here, the two of us," Cameron said. "I know the idea pains you, but how long can you tolerate this? Living with outlaws always around? Maybe you could sell the place. The people in Fortune must know it's a good little ranch."

"He wouldn't let us just up and ride out. We know where he is, Cameron. The law wants him."

"We could come up with a plan. Get you all gussied up and tell him we're going to find a preacher—that would fit in with what I already told him."

"Just trick him . . . pretend we're going to get married."

"Sure."

"Just pretend . . ." Then she spun away and walked into her bedroom, slamming the door, leaving Cameron to scratch his head, wondering what he'd said that was wrong.

It was ham and biscuits for supper and Cameron loaded three plates up with food, stuffed three forks in his pocket, and took the food across to the men who were in the barn, perched on the tailgate of the buckboard.

He gave each man a plate and then handed each a fork. "I hear you're getting hitched," Beeman said. Food clung to his matted black beard. His porcine eyes glared out at Cameron Black from beneath wild bushy eyebrows.

"That's right," Cameron said.

"When?"

"Soon," Cameron answered, realizing already that he was being baited. Perhaps it was some kind of initiation rite.

Perhaps they planned to kill him.

Either way he felt his body begin to tense, his senses to become more alert. Dan Beeman continued to chew his food open-mouthed, to stare at Cameron. The Kid just watched. There was amusement in Abel Packett's eyes.

"Not too soon, I hope," Beeman said, belching. "The rest of us want a crack at her too."

"Too late, friend, sorry," Cameron said coolly.

"Who said I was your friend?" Beeman demanded in a booming voice. He jerked involuntarily and a biscuit tumbled from his tin plate to land on the ground. All four of them stared at it as if it were a magic sign.

101

"Pick that up!" Beeman commanded. His tiny eyes grew smaller and still more malevolent.

"Not hardly," Cameron said. He knew they were testing him again, knew that there was a chance, and a good one, that it would come to blows; and he had no desire to fight the huge bearded man with the thick chest and shoulders that looked ready to split his shirt. But he couldn't back down, and still maintain their respect.

Beeman rose slowly to his feet, placing the tin plate behind him on the tailgate.

"I told you to pick up that biscuit, Black."

"What did I tell you? I won't do it. I'm nobody's servant. I work for Packett. I do what he tells me. I do what I want otherwise."

Beeman didn't tip it at all. Before Cameron Black could react at all a big fist shot out and caught him flush on the jaw. Cameron sprawled back on the ground and lay there, his head spinning. Lights flashed on in the back of his skull and there was sharp stabbing pain behind his left eye. Cameron struggled to shake it off and to rise on rubbery legs.

He got some help getting up.

Beeman grabbed him by the shirtfront and hoisted him to his feet; the big man's breath was rancid, his eyes fierce.

Cameron Black smashed his forehead against the bridge of Beeman's nose and with a howl the big man released his grip and stepped back, blood spewing from his broken nose.

"You son of a bitch," he growled and he drew his knife. Cameron had seen it coming and now he had the double-edge knife Cassie had given him in his hand. The two men had begun to circle and feint when Packett's voice bellowed.

"No! No, you damn fools!" It wasn't that Packett was against bloodshed in particular, but he was aghast at the thought of losing two of his men on the night before a job.

"I don't need it anyway," Beeman rumbled and he threw his knife aside.

Cameron Black dropped his as well. His head had had time to clear in the interim and now he waited, fists clenched, eyes alert, body crouched and ready.

Beeman tried the sucker punch again, but Cameron drew back and to one side and the right thudded painfully but relatively harmlessly off Cameron's shoulder.

Expecting that punch, Cameron was ready and as Beeman's heavy fist slammed into his shoulder he was able to counterpunch with an uppercut which buried itself in the big man's beard, driving the lower jaw of Beeman up savagely. A tooth in the outlaw's mouth cracked audibly.

Beeman roared with anger and threw himself at Cameron but Black stepped aside and tripped the onrushing outlaw and Dan Beeman went down on his face.

"You bastard," Beeman grumbled.

Cameron let him come up. He ducked a left and then stuck out three quick lefts of his own. The first one caught the big outlaw on his broken nose. The second straight left caught his eye. The third missed because Beeman was backing away snuffing and snorting as he tried to breathe through his broken nose.

For a moment Cameron thought he was through, but

he had misread Beeman. With a roar the big man charged Cameron Black again. Bearlike arms wrapped around Black and as he flailed away Beeman kept running, Cameron Black locked in his arms.

Black was jarred against the corral posts, the impact knocking the air from his body. Again he came close to going under. The horses whinied in fear and ran in circles, raising a choking dust cloud. Beeman slammed a meaty fist into Cameron Black's kidney and pain coursed through his battered body.

Woozily he tried to fight back but the big man seemed miles away. Beeman dropped his grip and wrapped his big hands around Cameron's throat, thumbs digging in. In desperation Black brought both hands up inside the grip, striking outward, breaking the grip. Then he dug a fist into the outlaw's soft belly and another to his ear. Dan Beeman backed away and Cameron followed him, throwing straight lefts and hooking rights which went over Beeman's tiring arms.

It was then that Beeman drew his pistol.

The shot rang out, rattling Cameron's ears, but it wasn't Beeman who had fired. Dust rose from the ground and both men turned their heads to see Abel Packett, smoking Colt in hand, standing there.

"That's enough. Dan, holster that revolver. Black— get back to the house."

Beeman, glowering, face bloody, slowly holstered his gun. Cameron stuck out his hand but Beeman turned his head and spat.

"Not hardly, Black," he said in a low hiss. "No one gets the better of Dan Beeman, no one! We'll finish this another time."

Then, as Black watched, the big man walked back to

the buckboard and slowly ground the biscuit into crumbs with his boot. Cameron turned and walked back toward the house where Cassie, hands to her mouth, watched from the porch.

"Cameron . . ."

"Out of here," he said, "we've got to get out of here."

Thirteen

They discussed it that night. The fire burned low again. In the barn the outlaws were hooting and shouting, loaded up on cheap whisky. The latchstring was in.

"You're right," Cassie said. "I can't be sentimental about it if you're going to get killed and I'm going to get . . . hurt."

"I agree. Consider this—we don't know how many more outlaws might show up here. Perhaps men even Packett can't control. You don't belong here, Cassie," he said, leaning forward to touch her hand.

"Where do I belong, Cameron?"

"Don't you have any relatives you could stay with?" he asked, and for a reason Cameron couldn't fathom, this seemed to annoy the woman.

"No," was all she said.

"Has Packett given you any money?" Cameron wanted to know.

"Tomorrow, he said."

"You'll at least have enough to get to a larger town."

"And do what?" she asked miserably. "Ranch life is all I know. Cameron . . .?" Her heart was aching to ask him, to tell him the things he seemed to be too busy to understand. Instead she just shook her head.

"What?"

"Be careful tomorrow, that's all."

"I intend to be," he replied with a smile. "Think about what I told you. If we can convince Packett we're going into town to find a preacher we can just keep riding."

"Maybe . . ." She paused for a long while before asking, "Do you think you'll ever get married, Cameron—after Susan?" Her eyes were on the embers in the fireplace and not on his.

"I don't know," he answered. "Could be, I guess." Then he stretched and yawned, announcing, "I guess I'd better get some sleep. I'll be doing some long riding come morning."

"All right." She rose, still not meeting his eyes. "I'll let you get some rest. I'll see you in the morning, Mr. Black."

Cameron watched her slim back as she walked toward the kitchen and her bedroom beyond. Mr. Black? Why did she call him that? A dim light went on in the back of his mind and then suddenly grew brighter as if someone were turning up the wick.

She couldn't mean . . . He frowned and then smiled faintly, a smile which turned into a grin wide enough to hurt his mouth. "Why you damn fool, Cameron Black," he said to himself. "You damn fool."

The knock on Cassie's door frightened her. She wore only her chemise and she grabbed her dress, holding it in front of her.

"Who is it?" she asked.

"The man who wants to marry you," Cameron Black answered, and she flung open the door, dropping her dress and clinging to him as he stroked her hair and held her tightly, both of them talking at once, apologizing, making vows, promising love.

Cameron was still in a daze when, ten minutes later, he returned to the front room. He had meant to get plenty of sleep that night—but there were plenty of other nights to come when he could catch up on his sleep. For tonight he just sat, watching the moon rise, amazed at his own lack of perception, overwhelmed by his good luck.

They would get out of there. Get out and travel long and far until they found a place no one had ever heard of Cameron Black, where they could work honestly all day, sleep together through the nights, and build a family and a future.

Nothing could stop them, no one. Cameron Black swore it. He would not allow anything to stand in their way.

The man with the black eye was friendly, Jake Weems thought. He had even given him a dime for lemon drops. Simon Black was slowly canvassing the town, certain in his own mind that if Cameron wasn't there, someone must have seen him. He must have stopped for supplies, at least for water.

He had split his men up. Campo had returned, finding no sign of a single rider farther up the trail. Now they had spread out across the town, making casual inquiries.

Simon had wandered over to the blacksmith's shop, thinking perhaps Cameron Black had had the gray's shoes renailed after its long run.

Then he had met young Jake Weems.

Normally Simon Black had no liking for kids. They were useless and always in the way. Just now, however, it behooved him to try to charm everyone he met. They sat perched on a fence rail as the smith looked over the gray horse's shoes.

"You ever seen that horse before, kid?" Simon Black asked.

"No, I don't think so."

The kid hesitated too long. He didn't look at Simon, but kept staring down at the dime which glittered in his palm. He wanted to be out of there, to run over to the general store and get a sack of lemon drops.

"You know why I ask?" Simon Black said, pressing on. "You seen those posters around town offering a reward for an outlaw?"

"I seen 'em," Jake Weems said, his interest rising some now.

"Well, I'm after him. I'm a marshal out of Tucson. This man's a murderer, and," he said nodding toward the gray, "that's his horse."

"A murderer!"

The kid's exclamation had its roots in more than excitement. Simon could detect fear in the boy's eyes and not just a youth's eagerness to hear tales of blood and daring.

"That's right. A stone cold murderer. Anyone who crosses him is bound to take a bullet. Sometimes he just kills for no reason at all."

Simon had guessed right—it was stark fear he had seen in Jake Weems's eyes. The killer was staying with Cassie Shore. He adored Cassie Shore, would do anything for her whether she paid him or not. Did she know the man was a murderer? No, how could she?

He almost blurted out what he knew to the marshal, but something caused him to hold back—the promise. He couldn't break his promise to Cassie Shore, but he couldn't let her get hurt either. The only solution seemed to be for him to ride out himself and warn her, to let her know she was sheltering a murderer.

The blacksmith, leading the gray, walked over to the fence.

"Nothin' the matter with those shoes, mister. I gave all the nails a tap just to make sure—won't charge you nothin' for that."

"And you've never seen that horse before?" Simon Black asked.

"No. Would've remembered. Nice-lookin' pony," the blacksmith said.

"All right." Simon's mouth tightened. He had wanted to talk to the kid some more—he was sure he knew something—and he had run out of excuses for remaining in the blacksmith's yard.

But it was no problem—there would be a time when the kid was alone. Then he could be questioned at length. Thoroughly questioned. If he knew something he wouldn't hold back long if Campo got ahold of him.

"I'd like to board it somewhere, where's best?" Simon Black asked.

"Best, I don't know. We only got one stable. See that green building across the way. Caffiter's Stable. He'll be glad for the business. Come on now, Jake. Give me a hand moving some of this iron stock."

The kid jumped down from the fence and the blacksmith, after a mistrustful glance at Simon, led the kid back to his shed.

Simon rode the gray up the street to the stable and made arrangements for the gray to be taken care of. He made inquiries there as well, but Caffiter had never seen Cameron or the gray horse either.

Simon stood in a narrow ribbon of shade beside the stable and stared out at the brown hills, sun-baked, rolling, forbidding.

He was running out of leads. It looked like Cameron had beaten them, like he had made his escape good. Still Simon had a gut feeling that he was in or near the town of Fortune. There was still the kid. He would have him watched, and when the time was right they would have an intimate talk with the Weems kid.

Cameron Black stepped out into the predawn gray and stood on the porch of the little house for a long minute before, carrying the half gallon coffeepot and three tin cups, he crossed to the barn.

The Kid and Beeman were still asleep in the bed of the buckboard which Cameron had provided with straw bedding and a tarpaulin sheet.

Abel Packett was up and dressed, cleaning his revolver. He nodded to Black and accepted a cup of coffee. Cameron put the pot and two remaining cups down on a nail keg.

"When?" Cameron asked.

"I'll kick their butts awake at first light. You're not drinking coffee?"

"I had two in the house. Didn't sleep much last night. I never do before a job," Black answered.

"Me neither," Abel Packett admitted. "You handled yourself pretty well with Beeman yesterday."

111

"Thanks. I wish you hadn't sicced him on me, though," Cameron said, and Packett grinned.

"You ain't dumb, are you?"

"You want dumb men riding with you?"

"No—you've got a point there. Muscle's fine, but there's times it takes smarts. One thing—I know Dan, he won't give it up. He thinks he's boss bear, and he's always pretty much proved it before."

"You can stop him," Cameron said.

"Yeah. I can stop him, but I won't always be around," Packett said.

"Well, then," Cameron said with a shrug, "I'll have to stop him."

Packett smiled, but his eyes examined Cameron Black as if he were seeing him for the first time. The man had confidence, and from what Packett had seen he knew Black was good enough with his hands. If he was as good with his guns, Packett was thinking he just might have found the lieutenant he had been looking for for a long time—a smart man, a tough man.

The only trouble with taking on a man like Cameron Black, Packett thought, was that he sometimes got a little ambitious and wanted to be top dog.

Black would stand some watching as time went along.

"I thought maybe some more of your men might have ridden in overnight," Black said.

"It looks like this is it for a while. Snow and Fann seem to be a lost cause. Don't worry. Word'll get out after we pull a few successful jobs. We'll have all the soldiers we need, I promise you."

They stood there in silence then until the first dull pink flush of dawn spread slowly across the eastern skies. Then Packett shook his men awake.

Beeman, growling and cursing, sat up, rubbing first his woolly head and then his belly. He saw Cameron Black then and, remembering, he gingerly touched his nose. His face was still caked with blood and the look in his eyes could have melted iron.

Still he said nothing. He slipped heavily from the makeshift bed and walked stiffly toward the water pump beside the house.

The Kid, by contrast, sat up and slipped from the wagon bed almost without sound, in one easy motion. He wiped back his thin blond hair with his fingers, and spying the coffeepot, poured himself a cup before putting on his faded, once black hat.

Packett let them each have a second cup of coffee before he said, "All right. Saddle up. It's a long ride, boys."

Cameron Black saddled the buckskin, which seemed eager to be out of the corral, meanwhile keeping an eye on Dan Beeman. The big man scowled at him but said nothing. Now was not the time for revenge anyway, Cameron knew. Not while there was a job to be done.

A "job." Robbing and perhaps killing some men. Cameron had considered just grabbing Cassie and taking off the night before—but that was close to impossible to accomplish. Even if no one was watching, to get the horses was unfeasible. Where would they have run?

It was better to stick to the original plan, to try it perhaps as soon as tonight. Cameron could pretend to be elated over the success of the job, if success it was . . . or he could be lying dead in the desert dust to leave Cassie at Packett's mercy.

They rode out with the glitter of the new sun lighting the tips of the cottonwoods, making a sinuous mirror of the creek. Vestiges of dawn color still clung to the horizon, scarlet and deep orange. There was a line of gold along the crests of the far hills.

They rode in a file, Cameron choosing to be the last man. He wanted no guns at his back if it could be helped.

Half an hour later they could see Fortune, and although they skirted it widely, they could hear a mule bray, the sound of hammer meeting anvil, the sharp, joyous cry of a boy and the barking of numerous dogs.

They rode directly into the sun for half an hour more until they reached the narrow canyon where deep, cooling shadows still covered the canyon floor. Cameron Black was reminded how much his life had changed since he had first ridden into the canyon, pushed that way by his trackers.

And where were they now? Had they given it up?

It was none too early to reach for his canteen and take a small swallow as they emerged from the canyon. On the desert floor beyond it was already warm. All signs of green vegetation fell rapidly away. Here and there were thorny mesquite or tall, whiplike ocotillo, not flowering now, and an occasional clump of saltbush, but for the most part there was only red sand desert for mile after mile until, far away, the Chocolate Mountains reared up, dead, convoluted, ancient.

No one spoke. They simply followed their leader onward toward the Butterfield grade, mile in the distance.

The Kid had slowed his horse a little and now he spoke to Cameron Black.

"Over there, you see that cut?" he asked, pointing toward a narrow break in the hills to the east. "That's Hollingsworth Pass. Follow it up and you come out above

114

the ranch. It's misery for a horse, but ain't nobody much knows about it or uses it except the 'paches."

"Doesn't it bother you?" Cameron asked. "Knowing that the Apaches are up there and Packett plans to ride through their territory?"

"Nothing much bothers me," the Kid said. Before Cameron had time to blink, the Kid drew his revolver, fired from the hip, and sent a small rock spinning into the air. A second shot caused it to explode in midair.

Packett swung around in his saddle. "Put that damn thing up!" he shouted.

"Sure, boss," the Kid said, and grinning, he holstered his pistol.

After another minute Cameron asked him, "Where are you from, Kid?"

"Tennessee. Some folks back there got fed up with me after I killed my second man. Came visiting with a rope. I decided to drift."

It was all very matter-of-fact. Most men would have embellished the tale with lurid detail. The Kid simply narrated the bare bones, yawned, and tugged his hat down against the glare of sun off the sand.

At ten o'clock they stopped at a small pool up a box canyon to let the horses rest and drink. A half a dozen palm trees clustered together as if for protection from the elements. The dry wind from out of the canyon rattled their fronds. It was the only water they had seen all morning, all they would see this afternoon.

They rode on sullenly, no one speaking. The wind began to pick up toward noon and they tied their bandannas across their faces to keep from breathing the blowing sand.

Shortly after noon they veered eastward again and

picked up the Butterfield grade. To the west was the tiny town of Boron, now invisible.

The winding stage trail switched back along the gorges, making its way up three thousand feet to the mesalike crest. There the stage driver usually halted his team to let them breathe, and to let any passengers stretch their legs.

If Packett had his way, this stage wouldn't make it that far. He led his soldiers up five hundred feet or so to where the trail made its initial switchback against the face of the dark hills.

Above it at this point was at least two thousand feet of sheer cliff face, below was a sheer drop to the canyon floor. The angle of the trail was steep. A hollow in the cliff provided cover for men and horses.

Packett swung down and ground-hitched his horse. The others followed suit.

"Dan, get up front fifty feet or so. I'll stop the coach myself. Kid, keep to the hollow and step out as soon as you hear me give my stand and deliver. Take the shotgun rider first. Cameron, get back down the trail and find yourself a place where they can't see you. As soon as they come past you, come up from behind, keeping an eye out for any passengers with big ideas."

The men split up, heading for their assigned positions. Cameron found a group of boulders to conceal himself behind, and with the sun beating down, his bandanna masking his face, he crouched and waited. Waited for men to die.

Fourteen

The sun beat down hotly. Cameron Black was crouched behind the stack of boulders on the stage route and to him the sun was like hot needles penetrating his clothing, broiling the skin beneath. The rocks around him were as hot as irons fresh from the stove, too hot to touch, the heat radiating off them.

He looked continuously toward the desert floor below him, hoping to see dust from the Butterfield stage. They must have had trouble up the line, because they were already an hour late.

Packett would be fuming. Again the wild notion of escape flashed through Cameron Black's mind. He had been placed in the rearmost post. If he could get on Captain Jack, ride to Hollingsworth Pass, and reach the ranch he and Cassie might have a chance . . .

It was crazy and he knew it. If they didn't pick him off with a rifle before he went a hundred yards, Packett might figure he was riding to give the alarm, and break off the plan just to stop him. Then again, there were only two ways out of the hidden valley and Packett and his men would be able to watch both of them and lie in wait for Cameron and Cassie.

No, it was foolishness. He would just have to be patient a while longer, wait for the opportunity to present itself.

He saw his hand tremble slightly. Nothing but the time spent immobile or nearly so, he told himself; but it wasn't that.

It was fear.

Cameron Black had been a warrior all of his life, with knuckles, knives, and guns. He had been a cavalryman, a lawman, a street fighter—it wasn't that sort of personal fear. It was an uneasiness about being involved in some foul deed like this, a fear of being forced to watch innocent people be killed. All he could do was try to mitigate the violence somehow.

His instinct, if any of the outlaws tried to kill anyone, would be automatic, deadly. Then he too would be cut down. But there was no way out now. He had been herded into this like a steer driven up a cattle chute. Looking back he still saw no way he could have avoided the tangle he was in, but that did nothing to ease the moral load he was carrying.

He saw it then—out on the desert flats, a plume of dust rising against the sky. There was a dark form before it as if the coach was trying to escape from some dust demon.

Cameron's mouth was dry, his tongue sticking to his palate. He took another drink of water and watched for what seemed like days as the coach trundled toward the grade.

Someone upslope whistled a signal in case one of them had failed to see the approaching Butterfield stage. One of the horses nickered at the sound and Cameron Black

118

heard Packett utter a muffled curse.

The coach was only a toy on the desert and then it suddenly disappeared, temporarily out of sight as it reached the bottom of the hill around the bend.

Now the driver would stop his horses, possibly rest them for a few minutes before beginning the long, slow haul up the grade.

It was quite a while later—too much later or too soon—that Cameron, his body stiff and hot, heard the chinking of trace chains, the squeak of springs, the popping of a whip, the clattering of hooves as the team struggled to draw the coach up the steep grade.

Cameron ducked even lower, removing his hat as he caught sight of the lead horses rounding the bend. His eyes searched the stagecoach quickly.

The driver and shotgun rider were in the boot. The shotgun was young, dozing, weapon propped up between his knees. The driver was older, red-faced, constantly popping his whip above the horses' heads. There were, thankfully, no passengers.

They passed Cameron very slowly, the yellow spokes of the wheels seeming hardly to rotate. He let it go on another ten feet then stepped into the road, wondering how he was going to react, what the end of this brutal scheme might be.

Packett's voice rang out clearly, echoing down the canyon. Cameron raced upslope, his heart pounding.

"Stand and deliver!"

And then the gunshot as the Kid took the shotgun rider. Cameron saw it all at once, a confused, violent tableau; Packett in front of the coach, just to the side of the wheel horse, gun leveled at the driver, who held trembling hands high; Beeman, grinning maliciously,

119

emerging from the hollow, gun pointed at the doors to the coach; the Kid, smoke still curling from his gun, racing toward the coach.

Why was he running? Then Cameron saw him. The shotgun rider had been hit but not killed. Dropping his weapon he had scrambled from the boot—or perhaps he had fallen. Now he was racing down the face of the cut below the road, angling toward Cameron Black, his face a mask of panic.

He was within fifty feet of Black and Cameron managed to catch his eye. In terror the shotgun rider scrambled on over the rough ground for a moment more before he realized that Cameron Black was signaling him to get down.

Out of desperation he obeyed, diving to the rocky, cactus-studded earth as Cameron Black simultaneously fired a shot deliberately high and wide.

The Kid had rounded the stage and was still on the run, gun in hand.

"I got him," Cameron said. "Let's see what kind of payday we got."

The kid nodded, holstering his gun. They returned to where the panicked driver had thrown down the strongbox to the two masked men who had their guns trained on him.

Packett stepped aside and growled. "Get out of here, driver. Get out and count yourself lucky you wasn't carrying a gun."

The driver in a frenzied flurry of motion grabbed for his whip, violently striped the flanks of his lead horses, and continued to strip them as the stage crept upgrade and was lost from sight. They saw it minutes later on the switchback, making as much time as it could, the driver still flailing the abused horses with his whip. Packett laughed and finally put his gun away.

"You got the shotgun, didn't you?" he asked the Kid.

"Black finished him," the Kid said. "Can't understand why I didn't drill him first shot."

"Can't either. Good work, Black," Packett said, "Let's crack the box and split it here. Makes for easier riding. Beeman, get that bar out of my saddlebags."

Dan Beeman went to Packett's horse and returned with a two-foot length of steel rod. This was placed through the lock hasp and Beeman jumped on the end of the rod. The second time, the lock sprang open and Packett moved to the small strongbox.

A few bills, some bonds, and what they had hoped for, a quantity of gold money in a number of different bags, each with a tag identifying the shipper.

Packett looked up with a wolfish grin. "A good take, boys," he said.

"Split it," Dan Beeman said, and Packett did.

As gang leader he put aside one bag as his own before he started dividing the small bags of gold evenly. Two bags to Dan Beeman, two to the Kid, and one to Cameron.

"Full cut for you next time, Cameron," Packett promised.

"That's all right. This will hold me for now. When do we work again?"

"We're going to have to lay low for a few weeks anyway—if there's too much activity around the ranch they'll start to close in on us. I mean to stay there for a while and see if the other boys don't show up before we start ranging far afield."

Stuffing their prizes in their saddlebags, they mounted. It felt good to have the bandanna off, good to be over with this, Cameron thought. Good to be heading back toward Cassie. He had gotten away with it today; but it had to be ended. Now. More outlaws coming in, more shooting, more men hurt or killed . . . it had to be finished.

He let the others ride out first, pretending to adjust the cinches on the Texas-rigged saddle Captain Jack carried. When they were around the bend in the trail he unlooped his canteen from his pommel and rode near to the rim of the trail. Then he flung it downslope to where the shotgun rider still feigned death.

Poor bastard—wounded with miles of desert to cross. He'd be lucky to make it. Maybe though if the Kid's bullet hadn't hit a vital area, with the water, if he could stick to the stage trail and be found before he bled to death, he would survive.

"Sorry," Cameron Black whispered, "it's all I can do." Then he nudged Captain Jack with his heels and the buckskin started down the trail, catching up with the others as they reached flat ground and the trail home.

The Kid asked Dan Beeman, "What're you going to do with your cut, Dan?"

"Go into Fortune—they got no warrant on me—and get quietly drunk."

"No trouble," Packett warned, "we don't need it."

"I said 'quietly,' boss," Beeman said.

"Sounds good to me," the Kid said, "mind if I come along?"

"Don't mind a bit. Why'n't you leave your gun, though?"

"Go in nekked?" The Kid was aghast.

122

"I seen you with a load on before. Like the boss says, we can't afford no trouble."

"All right," the Kid agreed. "I'll leave my gun and be a good boy too. There any loose women in that town?"

Packett said, "They got a saloon, don't they?" All three men laughed at that. "Hell, flash a few dollars and buy a few drinks—that's all it takes."

The Kid said, "What about you, Cameron?"

"Me?" Black grinned. "Boys, if we ain't going to work for a while, I'm going to go over to Boron and get myself hitched."

Packett's head came around, his face tight. He didn't like the idea of Cameron riding out. He started to forbid it, but gave himself time to think it over.

Cameron Black had proved today that he wasn't a ringer. When the Kid had missed the shotgun rider, Black hadn't shown any qualms about finishing the job. And he had seen the poster on Black. Besides, the woman wasn't going to ride off and leave her ranch to Packett. Nor could she open her mouth without losing her income and ultimately the ranch.

At the bottom Packett had to admit that there was another reason he objected—he had wanted Cassie Shore for a long time as his own woman. It was obvious now that she wanted Black and only by putting Black out of the way could he break that up. Then he would be left with some whining, sobbing girl.

Hell, it wasn't worth it. Let them do what they wanted—he would get drunk with the boys, and, as he said, buy some skirt a few drinks and get what he needed in town.

"Luck, Black," he said grudgingly. "Make sure you're back in a week."

123

"I'll be back. Hell, I'll probably be broke by then once Cassie gets to shopping."

There was a faint appreciative chuckle from the Kid and Packett nodded. Even Dan Beeman seemed in a relatively good mood now that there was gold in his saddlebags. They rode southward, aiming their horses toward Hollingsworth Pass and the ranch.

Fifteen

They made the ranch in late afternoon. The horses were weary, the men trail-sore. They had ridden a rough road through the heat of day, but they counted themselves the most fortunate men on earth. They had seen no Apaches, and they had made two months' wages or more for a day's work.

Cassie hadn't seen them until they came down out of the sandhills. Then she rushed out of the house, a frying pan still in her hands, and ran to Cameron even before the horses had stopped. He pulled up and swung down, holding her tightly.

"You're all right?" she asked, touching him as if to assure herself he wasn't an apparition.

"All right."

"Thank God. Cameron . . . we can't let this happen again," Cassie said.

"It won't," Black said positively. The outlaws had continued on to rub down their horses, corral them, and see to their hay and water.

"How can you be sure?" she asked, her eyes still wide

with emotion.

He kissed her once, and drew away, his arms still locked around her. "Because we're leaving tonight. We're going to ride to Boron, get married, and keep going."

"Cameron!"

"Changed your mind?"

"No, but, will . . .?"

"Packett gave me an okay. He has no reason to think we'd run out on him, and if we did, what is it he thinks we could do? I can't turn him into the law. To his way of thinking I'm an outlaw too . . . Maybe I am now," he added glumly.

"It's scary, Cameron, really scary."

"Yes, it is, Cassie. Not as scary as staying here might become, I'm thinking. Let me put Captain Jack up and we'll talk."

"All right, yes," she said, jabbing at her hair with her fingertips in a nervous gesture, "don't be long though Cameron, will you?"

"Not long, I promise." He kissed her again and reluctantly let his arms drop away. Cassie yelled across to Packett.

"I've got some steaks and grits! You boys holler when you're ready!"

"Bring 'em on!" Packett yelled back, and he actually seemed to be wearing a genuine smile on his wolfish face. Well, why not? He was out of jail, pockets bulging with gold, looking forward to a good meal and, later, whisky and a piece of fluff. Yeah, he was in a good mood—but he might not be for long. Now, Cameron knew, was definitely the time to do it. Gather a few of Cassie's things up and ride. Start all over again somewhere. Anywhere at

126

all. It would work with this woman.

Cameron put Captain Jack up, grooming him, pitching him some hay. In the barn the outlaws were whooping it up, reliving the day and past days. One of them had had a bottle of whisky and now as Cameron passed the barn door, the Kid offered it to Black.

"You done as much as any of us. Drink to the Packett gang."

"Gladly," Cameron said, wiping the top of the bottle with his sleeve. "And to friends," he said, looking at Beeman, who gave him the slightest nod of acknowledgment. Cameron drank from the bottle, handed it back, and started toward the pump, where he removed his shirt and soaked his head and torso in cold water.

He helped Cassie deliver the steaks and hominy grits to the outlaws, who were still celebrating the job, then together they returned to the house, closing the door behind them.

"You mean it, don't you Cameron—we're going tonight. And," she asked almost cautiously, "we're going to get married?"

"We're leaving tonight, yeah," Cameron said. He started toward the kitchen. "This my steak on the table . . ." He spun. "And we're going to get married, if you'll have me, woman!"

Cassie leapt into his arms, squeezing his neck tightly. "You tease!" she exclaimed. "You darn dirty coyote tease!"

They sat together at the table. Cassie was too nervous to eat much, but the long day had left Cameron with a big appetite.

"When, Cameron?"

"I'd like to wait until after they leave. They're riding

127

into town to celebrate. But if we wait until then we won't have daylight to see us down Hollingsworth Pass."

"We're going that way?" Cassie asked. "What about the Indians?"

"We didn't see any sign of them on the way up. I hope they've cleared out of the area. I can't ride through town—not if there's a chance those men are still waiting for me, and the more I think of that, the more I think it's a strong possibility.

"They can't know about Hollingsworth. As soon as we get to the flats, we've got it made. Do you know that place with the pool and the palm trees?"

"Palm Canyon, yes," she answered.

"I figure we can make it that far before dark. Come morning we can beeline it toward Boron. Then we're safely gone."

Cassie was worried, but she was a lot of woman and she nodded positively. "All right, if that's the way you've planned it, that's the way we'll do it. I trust my man to solve things."

"What about after we're married?" Cameron asked with a smile.

"Then, too, husband. Then too." She kissed his cheek and started cleaning off the table before she stopped herself and said, "What am I bothering to do this for?" She looked around the house, remembering many things, saying good-bye to her past.

"What can I take?"

"Not the furniture," Cameron said lightly. "Things you need, special things. We can't take a packhorse— that would look too suspicious to Packett. Sorry, Cassie, I know I'm asking you to give up a lot for me."

128

"Cameron. I'd give up my life for you," she said, and she meant it. She was quite a woman, Cassie Shore. He tried the sound of her new name in his mind, liking it just fine: Cassie Black.

He finished eating while she rummaged through her bureau and packed as many clothes as she thought practical. In the barn the hooting had become louder, the laughter more raucous.

"I'm going to test Packett's mood again, Cassie. Keep packing."

She appeared in the doorway, folding a dress. "You think that's a good idea?" she asked.

"Yes, I do. I want to keep him thinking I'm a member of the gang, that I think they're a grand bunch of men, that I'm thrilled by their company."

"If you think so. I just don't like it."

"At least you don't have to smell them," Cameron said. He looked out the window. "Not a lot of sun. Enough to reach the flats, I think. Half an hour, Cassie."

"All right . . . Cameron, I'm still scared. My stomach is all in a knot."

"Mine too, Cassie, but it'll be all right, it has to be. Tell me," he said, thinking of something after he had risen, "is there any liquor in this house?"

"What for?" she asked. "Oh, I see. Dad used to keep a jug of corn liquor in the cupboard below the sink there, to the left . . . Find it?"

"Yup." Cameron rose and shook the jug, which seemed about a third full. He pulled the cork and smelled it. It was nasty-smelling stuff, but it should do the job. He put on his hat and went across to the barn.

Expansively he called to the men in the barn, waving

129

the jug in the air.

"Okay boys!" he called coming toward them with a slight, assumed stagger. "Drink one to me and Cassie. We're leaving today. When we come back they'll be a Mrs. Black!"

He handed the jug to Packett, who took it and drank deeply, too grateful for the liquor to question Cameron's reason for leaving immediately.

The Kid drank next, lifting the jug to the house and then to Black. "Luck to you—here's to the beautiful future Mrs. Black and to Cameron—the only man who's outshot the Kid lately."

He drank deeply and passed it to Dan Beeman, whose scowl softened as he said, "And here's to you both—and the man who *damn near* whipped me." He must have put a half-pint down at a pull.

Cameron shook hands all around, then shook hands all around again like any slightly tipsy bridegroom at his bachelor party. Then with a hiccup he said, "Got to saddle up. You boys don't tear that poor little town down tonight now."

"They're safe," the Kid said, and he patted his empty holster. That got a laugh and the jug was passed again as Cameron grabbed Cassie's blanket, bridle, and saddle and staggered to the corral, his face, now that they could no longer see him, a disgusted mask.

He saddled her bay quickly, then turned toward Captain Jack. Logic told him to leave the buckskin and take a fresher horse, but the big horse had memories for Cassie and him both.

"Can't leave you behind, big fellow," Cameron said, and he swung the blanket onto the buckskin's back.

He walked the horses back to the house, enduring

catcalls and whistles. He gave them a friendly wave and a fake grin and walked on, trying to appear casual, unhurried. His nerves were jumping badly. Nothing could go wrong now, but he wanted out of there, off that ranch, away from the Packett gang. And he wanted to be gone *now*.

"Cassie!" he called.

"Ready," she said. She was breathless, shaken.

"Let's go! Now. What can I take?"

"I've got all I'm taking in here," she said. She had two burlap bags tied together at their tops. These could be slung like saddlebags over the horse haunches. "I've got your spare clothes too. Have you got your rifle?"

"Yes. A canteen?"

"I filled two—in the kitchen."

"You're a wonder, lady," Black said appreciatively.

"A few provisions, a few dresses, my husband—it's all I really need, Cameron." Still she looked around the house wistfully before she said a little sharply, "Let's go, I'm ready."

"Play up to the boys," Cameron said and she nodded her understanding. She took a deep breath and put a smile on her face. They went out then, waving and calling out good-byes while the outlaws, half-drunk, whistled and yelled any profane comment that came to mind.

Cameron let Cassie mount and while she sat there smiling and waving, he tied the burlap sacks on, swung aboard Captain Jack, and with the outlaws' jeers still ringing in their ears, rode out of the ranch forever.

Half a mile on Cassie stopped her horse and buried her face in her hands, crying. Cameron backed Captain Jack and looped a long arm around her shoulders.

"Cassie?"

"I'm all right," she said, looking at him with tearful eyes. She sniffled and looked back down the road. "We made it, Cameron!" she said ecstatically. "We actually made it!"

"We did," he answered with a smile. "Come on, now, let's put some distance between us and them. A lot of distance."

Sixteen

The Kid had some trouble getting off his horse. One boot had slipped all the way through the stirrup as he attempted to dismount. His other foot hit the ground in front of the Caribou Saloon and he lurched against his roan horse, his fuddled mind trying to sort out what was happening.

Beeman and Packett laughed uproariously. The Kid had never been a good drinker, and the corn liquor Black had given them had done a good job on the Kid.

Packett himself was in grand spirits. He was king of his own world, warmed by liquor, his coffers filled with stolen gold.

Beeman helped the Kid disentangle himself and together the three men stepped up onto the sagging plank porch of the Caribou. Inside music played on a tinny piano and men shouted. Glass tinkled and a single loud crash echoed through the night.

Packett paused at the batwing doors to peer into the smoky interior. A man couldn't be too cautious. He saw no one he knew, no one who looked as if he might be toting a badge. Anyway, he and Beeman were wearing their guns. Anyone wanting to take them down would have hell to pay.

The Kid was by far the best of them with a gun, but when he drank he was unpredictable. In Waco once he had bet a man he could pick off every shot glass on the bartender's shelf one by one. He had gotten twelve in a row before the local law showed up. Fortunately the hick marshal didn't know who he had under lock and key and Packett and Snow had bailed him and ridden out. From that day on Packett had refused to allow the Kid a gun in a saloon.

The Kid was good because he loved weapons. They were his favorite toy, his passion. He could buy a hundred rounds and burn them up contentedly in some canyon, wasting the day away.

To Packett a gun was a tool, protection and a way to make a living. He shot when he felt the need—perhaps that was why he would never be as good as the Kid. No matter, he was good enough. He was still walking around, and there were plenty who had tried to put him down who weren't.

"Well?" Beeman demanded impatiently. The big man was thirsty.

"We go in. No fights, Dan."

"I'm only here for the whisky and the women," Beeman assured his boss.

Beeman, slightly drunk himself, still understood as Packett did, that they couldn't afford any trouble. They had a cozy setup at the Shore ranch and the last thing they needed was to be forced to go on the run at this time.

Not that Beeman would swallow an insult at any time. Fortunately his sheer size was intimidating and not many men wanted to challenge him.

They pushed on through the doors, a scattering of glances coming their way. The three made their way to the bar, where Packett bought a bottle of rye from a balding, perspiring bartender; then, looking around, they went to a corner table where they settled in, the Kid tilted back against the wall, hat over his eyes.

Packett nudged Beeman as a woman in a flaming red dress with black ruffles swished past, giving them a tantalizing, professional smile.

Beeman reached out to grab her, but she twisted away.

"Not just yet, big man," she said. "But I'll be back."

Packett said, "Black don't know what he's missing out on. Man shouldn't limit himself to one skirt, I always said." A part of that was sour grapes, but Packett believed it. The more he thought about losing Cassie Shore, the more he counted himself lucky. The girl was straitlaced and would want her old man tied down good and proper.

Packett put down a healthy drink and poured himself another. The black-eyed man at the next table was watching him. When he spoke, Packett barely heard him the first time.

"Pardon me," the black-eyed man repeated.

Packett's eyes shifted that way, as did Beeman's, instantly suspicious. Their profession mandated suspicion. The black-eyed man sat at a table with a redheaded man, a lantern-jawed man with a sandy mustache, and a broad-shouldered Swede. They were a tough-looking crew, but the one with the black eyes was well-spoken.

"What?" Packett growled. His hand had already dropped to his lap to be nearer his Colt.

"I thought I heard you mention a man named Black," the stranger said.

Packett grew cautious. You didn't admit anything if

135

you didn't know whom you were talking to, especially not if someone was asking about a member of your own gang. He shook his head.

"You must've heard wrong," Packett snarled. He drank again and inclined his head to one side, gesturing to Beeman. They nudged the Kid and the three of them moved to another table.

"What do you make of that?" Cummings said, scratching his arm.

"I know he said 'Black,'" Simon said.

"Plain as day," Forrest agreed.

"So Cameron *is* around somewhere still."

Wally Kirk stroked his long jaw and tugged thoughtfully at his mustache. "But how in hell could he have hooked up with those three? Who the hell are they, anyway?"

"I have no idea," Simon Black said. His brother was basically a loner; and if he was trying to hide out, it was odd he would be known to these three. They didn't look like cowhands, miners, or sheepherders. "What did you make of them, Dominguez?" Simon Black asked the Mexican.

"What do you think? Outlaws, Simon. I don't know who they are, but you tell me, what else could they be?"

Simon shook his head in puzzlement. His brother was a straight arrow. So far as Simon knew his brother had never broken a law in his life. It was inconceivable that Cameron Black could be riding with outlaws. Yet he felt strongly that Dominguez had pegged these three correctly. He had noted the way they moved, the way they carried thier guns, the way their eyes were constantly moving, the way they gravitated toward the corner tables, keeping their backs to the wall.

He couldn't fathom it all, but he was convinced of one

thing: Cameron Black was still in the area. Casually, Simon went to the bar and, ordering another bottle of whisky, asked the balding bartender. "Those three in the corner, do you know who they are?"

"Why are you asking me, friend? I don't know anything. I serve drinks."

He left Simon there for a minute while he drew two beers, served them, and dropped the nickles into the cash register. When he wandered back toward where Simon Black stood, a foot on the brass rail, he noticed the gold eagle on the bar and his eyes gleamed as brightly as the ten-dollar coin. Without a word he scraped the coin off the bar and pocketed it. He was suddenly more outgoing.

"What was it you wanted, sir? Clean glasses?" he asked too loudly.

"I wanted to know who those three men in the corner are."

"I'll look in the back. I don't know if we have it. Would you like to see?"

Simon winced. The bartender was a terrible actor. He motioned to Dominguez to come and get the bottle and glasses. Then he sauntered toward the back room, following the bartender, imagining the eyes on his back from the corner table.

It didn't matter. He had to know.

The back room was a jumble of beer barrels, empty and full, whisky bottles, stacks of empty crates, and at least one rat.

It was stifling in there and the sweating bartender toed the sawdust on the floor nervously. "I don't know much, mister. What I do know I'll tell you quick."

"All right—tell me," Simon Black said.

"The tall one. He used to come in here a lot, but I haven't seen him for a year or so. The big one was usually with him, and a couple of other hard-looking men. They'd not show for a week or two and then they'd be here every night and sometimes every day too for a week or even a month. Then they'd drop out of sight again. They spend a lot of money. They used to tip the girls maybe ten dollars a night. Like I say, I haven't seen them for maybe a year. I'm glad they're back, but I always have that feeling, you know, that something's going to happen sooner or later. That's all I know. I hope it was worth your ten bucks. Now I got to get back behind that bar."

Simon, his brow furrowed in puzzlement, watched the bartender go out. He stood in the dim room for a moment, thinking. The rat, or another, scuttled past again and Simon Black kicked at it. Then he went back to his table.

"Well?" Wally asked without looking up. The second bottle was nearly gone, which surprised Simon not at all. All of them, Cummings, Dominguez, Forrest, and Wally, were big drinkers.

"They're outlaws, for sure," Simon replied. "They ride out for weeks or months and come back with big money. But what in hell is Cameron doing with them!" His voice was soft but there was tension in it, the tension that comes from frustration, the inability to solve a puzzle which should be simple but whose solution is tantalizingly elusive.

There was nothing else to do just then but have another drink. He knew that approaching the party of outlaws would have no positive result.

He could only hope that the Indian's work would fill in the rest of the puzzle.

Campo watched patiently. The small house was already lighted though it was not yet dusk. Smoke rose from the stone chimney. He was squatted down in the screening sage and sumac bordering the yard of the house, his eyes on the back window and door. Once in a while he saw the heavy woman moving past the window, and from time to time his quarry, the kid.

Campo was in no hurry at all. Things happen or they don't. There is success or there isn't. No man can speed things up or slow events down. One waited, one watched; if opportunity presented itself, one acted.

Campo was a quiet man, a patient man, slow-moving except when circumstances demanded action. There was no sense in worrying, there was no sense in fearing anything, even death. Every man's time came.

He was a Delaware Indian. Once, for a period of five years, after his own people had kicked him out, he had scouted for the army. Then he had made the mistake of killing a lieutenant who had insulted him. Now he was among friends, men who understood his motives. You accept no insults; you kill when it must be done.

Simon Black wished to kill his brother—why, Campo did not fully understand, except that it involved a woman. . . . White women were much trouble, Campo decided. They believed themselves the equal to a man. . . .

The back door suddenly opened and Campo lowered his head, hearing the heavy white woman's voice.

"And make it a good load unless you want to eat your dinner cold, Jake."

"Yes, Ma," the boy said.

He was probably twelve or thirteen years old. As he closed the door he made an angry gesture toward the kitchen and stalked off toward the woodpile in the corner of the yard.

Campo moved.

Through the shadows, through the scratchy brush

139

which clutched at him with scraggly fingers, Campo moved toward the woodpile as well, and when the boy, an armful of wood clutched to him, looked up, it was already too late. Campo was there, ready to clamp a hand over Jake Weems's mouth and drag him struggling off into the brush beyond the yard.

The Delaware threw the kid over the withers of his horse and drew his knife, holding it in front of the frightened boy's eyes.

"Now," Campo said, "we will talk."

He rode a mile north, toward the town, and dismounted in a copse of willow brush along the creek. Jake held absolutely still until the Delaware grabbed him by the belt and pulled him to the ground, where he landed roughly.

"What . . . what do you want?" Jake asked. Campo crouched down in front of him, running a finger along the edge of the knife blade.

"I want the murderer," Campo said. "He has killed my squaw. Now I must kill him before he kills again. My knife," he said dramatically, "craves blood . . . any blood."

Jake Weems was quivering with fear. He sat in the darkness staring up at the Indian, who was only a shadow before the moon, a terrible, demonic creature with glinting steel in his broad hand.

"I don't know any murderer," Jake said weakly.

"You know, boy," Campo said, leaning closer still, "and if you do not tell me, perhaps my knife will find the blood it craves right here on this night."

Seventeen

The bartender's head snapped up. The man who strode through the door was an Indian. He wore a shirt with a zigzag pattern in red and green against a black background, black jeans, fringed boots, and a high-crowned black hat with a small hawk feather in the band.

It was illegal to serve an Indian still in the territory, but the bartender had no inclination to try to deny him entrance to the saloon, especially after he saw that he was walking to the table where the four hardcases sat. He got back to polishing his glasses. Something was going on on this night, but the bartender decided he didn't want to know what it was. The less a man knew sometimes, the better off he was.

Campo pulled up a chair, grabbed the bottle of whisky, and took a long pull before he nodded to Simon Black.

"We got him," Campo said.

"The kid talked?"

"What do you think?" Campo asked with a broken-toothed smile.

"You didn't hurt him did you?" Forrest asked.

141

"No. What for? Made him wet his pants a little, though," Campo said, chuckling at the memory.

"All right," Simon said irritably, "forget the kid's welfare—what did he tell you about Cameron Black?"

Campo took another drink and leaned forward. "There's a ranch west of town. The Shore ranch he called it. A woman who lives out there paid the kid a dollar to take the gray horse up over that gap they call Rattlesnake Canyon. She made him promise not to tell anyone."

"Then the ranch is where Cameron went."

"That's the kid's guess although he hasn't been down there since that day."

"Where else would he go?" Wally asked. "He's charmed some woman and she's putting him up."

Simon Black was turning the entire proposition over in his mind. It didn't quite fit together.

"Where do those three come in?" Simon wondered, nodding toward the three men in the corner who had begun whooping it up in earnest. The one with the black beard had a saloon girl in a yellow dress on his lap. "Why would they know about Cameron?"

"No one else did."

"They have to be staying out at the ranch too," Forrest guessed. "Maybe they're cowhands after all."

Simon let out a short, explosive laugh. "Not from what I've heard, not from what I see."

"I agree," Dominguez said. "And you know, I think I've seen that tall one before somewhere," he added, meaning Packett.

"Where?" Simon asked with interest.

"I can't quite remember, boss. Just one of those faces you recall without really knowing from where."

142

"What do you want to do?" the big man, Cummings, asked around his cigar.

"Do? Get down to that ranch. Did you get directions, Campo?" The Indian nodded. "Then let's go. Let's find Cameron Black."

Packett looked up as they tramped past and out the batwing doors. His scowl was deep. There was something he didn't like about that bunch. Were they looking for Black? Why, if so?

They sure as hell weren't lawmen, not with a Mex and an Indian with them, no badges showing. . . . Packett got to his feet. He walked toward the door, watching Simon Black's men mount. What if they *were* lawmen? Maybe rangers, maybe just an informal posse. What if the stage driver had somehow recognized Cameron Black during the holdup?

So long as they stayed out of Packett's territory, he didn't care. Black was a good enough gunhand, he was part of the gang, but Packett had no particular love for him—he had never loved any man, woman, or animal. So long as the men stayed away from Packett himself, he didn't care.

And Packett was far from unobservant. He had seen the black-eyed man go into the back room with the bartender, seen the nervous way the bartender had looked at him afterward. The man had been asking too many questions. Packett didn't like this at all.

So long as they stayed out of his area . . .

Then he saw the strangers ride to the end of town and turn west.

And the only thing to the west was the Shore ranch.

Packett slammed his hand against the door frame. He spun on his boot heel. Beeman was busy tickling his saloon girl anyplace she'd let him tickle her. The Kid was tilted against the wall, half-drunk, half-asleep. Packett walked up to a lean man in a checked shirt and suspenders who was talking to the bartender.

"Friend?" Packett said, and the man turned toward him. "How much did you pay for that Colt you're wearing?"

After a moment's confusion, he said, "Why, fifteen bucks, but 'twasn't new."

"Will you take fifty dollars for it? Now."

"Fifty . . .?" The lean man looked at Packett as if he were crazy. "For fifty, mister, I'll throw in the belt and holster and my shirt."

"Keep your shirt," Packett said. "The rest I'll take." And he slapped two double-eagles and an eagle on the counter before the man's eyes.

The man shrugged, looked at the bartender, and then gave the maniac his gunbelt. Packett, without another word, walked to the table, kicked the Kid's chair, and tossed the gunbelt and the .44 Colt on the table. He yanked the girl from Beeman's lap and said:

"We've got trouble. Let's ride."

The Kid was suddenly alert. His eyes went to the gun. Beeman seemed instantly sober.

"What is it?" Dan Beeman asked.

"Outside. We're riding."

The bartender watched them go and thanked his God that wherever all of them were going he wasn't going to be there.

The night was warm. Only the slightest of breezes moved across the desert, shifting the fronds of the trees in Palm Canyon. The moon shone on the pool of water which burbled up from a deep spring and fed the trees and the wildlife that crept in from the desert and surrounding hills.

The man and the woman there had no fire, needed none. The moon was bright, the heat of the day lingering in the rocks and sand. They sat close together on an Indian blanket, Cameron's arm around Cassie, watching as a doe mule deer, fawn beside her, crept toward the pool to drink.

They did not move, they did not speak. They were together and the night was warm, the world was good. The deer drank and then wandered back onto the desert.

"We've made it," Cassie said. Her head was against his shoulder. For the first time that day she was able to relax.

"So it seems," Cameron Black answered. He too was relaxing finally. The ride through Hollingsworth Pass had been nerve-torturing, a torment for the mind. With the Packett gang behind them, with the possibility of Apaches lurking, Cameron, the safety of the woman entirely in his hands, had ridden as if into battle.

For he had taken this lovely lady away from her home and promised her better times, safety, love. He could not let her down; nor could he again go through the pain of losing a woman he loved now that he had finally found her.

"Do you think about her still?" Cassie asked as if reading his mind.

"I think about you," Cameron answered.

"Seriously?"

"Seriously."

"Cameron . . ." She looked at him, and her eyes were those of a child and a wise older woman at once. "You've never said it, you know."

"Haven't I?" he asked, knowing full well what she meant.

"No."

"Then I'll say it now—I love you, and only you and I will go on loving you and doing for you, Cassie Shore Black."

And they lay back on the blanket to hold and comfort each other through the long desert night.

Simon Black led his men westward. The trail was well marked in the dry grass of the valley, and the moon made traveling easy. He had quit considering the men in the saloon, the three hardcases. They didn't matter anymore.

Only killing Cameron Black mattered.

It was simple. If he didn't kill Cameron, his brother would kill him, or perhaps see that he was hung, which was even worse, although the end result was the same.

Ahead he could see the hills gradually becoming higher until they formed a broken bluff on either side of the valley. It couldn't be much farther, he knew. The desert itself couldn't be more than five miles on.

He began to feel an eagerness, something approaching joy. He had chased Cameron halfway across the territory, and now he was nearly within sight of his goal.

"Think there's another way out of here?" he asked Cummings.

The big man shook his head. "I don't know. It don't seem likely."

"I wonder if there's anyone else on the ranch?" Forrest said, an edge of nervousness in his voice.

146

"Probably," Wally said, "those three we saw in the saloon are all there are. All the men would have wanted to go into town."

"Cameron didn't," Dominguez said.

"He couldn't," Simon reminded him. "Besides, he's cozied up with some woman. He'd welcome the chance to be alone, I'm thinking."

"I hope he's in bed," Wally said. "I wouldn't want to try taking him if he is ready and waiting, no matter how many of us there are. I seen his work before."

"We'll take him this time, don't worry," Simon Black replied.

Damn right he'd take him. And if he was in bed with Susan . . . Simon shook his head. No, he had already taken care of Susan. This was a different tramp. Why did they always want Cameron? What did he have? His pockets were usually empty. Maybe he would find them in bed—the thought tantalized Simon Black. Let them die in the bed. Cameron and Susan . . . no, the other one. Then he would set fire to the place just like he did to the McCulloch house. Without knowing it, Simon was grinning, but it was a grotesque parody of pleasure. Forrest made the suggestion twice before Simon was aware that the redhead was speaking to him.

"What did you say?"

"Said, why don't we send a scout in when we reach the ranch instead of just riding up? One man who could maybe say he was looking for work. Or send Campo. He could work his way around the house and have a look-see."

"Maybe so," Simon agreed. "That's probably the way to go. We'll wait and see." He turned in his saddle.

147

"Don't forget, boys, the night Cameron Black goes down, there's a bonus for every one of you. Let's make it tonight."

Campo's hand suddenly shot into the air and he hissed, "Hold up!"

"What is it?" Simon asked, and then he too saw it. The valley floor suddenly widened and they could make out two structures ahead of and below them, a small house and a barn with corral attached. Cattle grazed or slept along the creek as it made a lazy bend through the cottonwood trees.

"That's it," Simon said. His chest was tight with emotion so that he could barely breathe. "It has to be."

"No lights," Campo said. "I don't see any damn lights down there."

"Don't need lights for what Cameron Black's doing," Forrest said.

"No sense in you going down, Campo," Simon said. "You won't be able to see a thing in the house through the windows. We'll send somebody—Forrest?—down to pretend he's a ranch hand looking for work. Can you handle it, Forrest?"

"Sure. He won't shoot me out of hand. I don't think he'll recognize me with this beard."

"Just don't shoot him," Simon said sternly. "Not yet."

"All right."

"We'll ride a little closer. I want to see him in that doorway, want to know we've got him. Campo—can you and Dominguez work your way around back in case he tries to run?"

"Sure, boss."

"I won't have him running. I won't let him run again."

148

The black-eyed man was speaking to no one. He was staring at the night, at the house, into his projected future, to where he was standing over the dead body of his brother, watching Cameron Black's pleading eyes, watching the blood seep from him.

"Let's go!" he said sharply, and as Forrest rode ahead toward the house, Campo and Dominguez started to ride in a half circle, splashing across the creek to cover the back of the house.

Simon Black gave them five minutes, and then he nodded to Wally and Cummings. "Let's get closer. It's almost over—finally over."

If he hadn't been so distracted, he might have heard the distant but audible sounds of horse's hooves pounding against the earth behind them; but he had only one thought in his mind—the death of Cameron Black.

Eighteen

"Slow 'em up," Abel Packett said, and they drew back on the reins of their horses. The ranch was close now. The tracks of the other riders were plain in the dew-moistened earth, in the grass beside the trail. "I don't want to spook them."

The night ride had cleared the Kid's head—that and the proximity of danger, which had sent a rush of adrenaline through his body.

"Who do you guess they are, Abel? Bounty hunters?"

"That's my first guess. They want that thousand on Cameron's head. But if they figure out who we are, they'll have a hell of a lot bigger payday than that," Packett responded.

"Cameron won't talk," the Kid said confidently.

"No, he won't. But if they put two and two together, they'll soon figure that we must be working the wrong side of the law too. If they check around a little—didn't you see that black-eyed man talking to the bartender?— they're liable to find out who we are, and there's good money on each of us.

"They can't live. It'll be a bitch of a bloody night, but they can't be allowed to live. Let's get off the trail, boys. We'll take the south trail. They can't know about that. Walk your horses, unlimber your guns. Cameron and Cassie are gone . . . everyone else is a target, right?"

Simon Black sat his horse fifty yards from the corral. His hand was cramped around his rifle and his eyes strained against the darkness. The moon sketched eerie shadows at the base of each corral post and made a pool of shadow in front of the house where Forrest had dismounted and was now walking to the door. Simon was bent forward at the waist, eagerness to kill drawing his body forward.

Beside him Wally's horse stamped its feet and blew. Wally let his eyes roam briefly, but he couldn't see Campo and Dominguez beyond the tree in the back of the house.

A moment later they could all clearly hear the sound of Forrest's knuckles rapping on the door to the house. Wally tensed, shot a glance at Cummings, and drew his rifle from its scabbard.

There was something he didn't like about this, but he couldn't put a name to it. No matter. This would be the night they took Cameron Black—no one man was going to stand against them, and with what he had earned so far on this manhunt plus the promised hundred-dollar bonus, he could ride out, have himself a damn good time, and do nothing but sit in the sun for a few months.

Forrest rapped again, but there was still no answer. They saw him turn and shrug, his palms spread. Simon Black was grinding his teeth together.

"Maybe he's not there after all," Cummings said.

Simon reacted angrily. "He's there, he's got to be. He just doesn't want to come to the door. He's in bed with Susan, having too much fun."

Wally looked again at Cummings, this time with a worried expression. Who the hell was Susan? The boss seemed to be on another planet. His mouth hung open and his eyes were glinting. A trickle of spit drooled from the corner of his mouth.

"Let's go. We're breaking in the house," Simon said abruptly. Wally wasn't crazy about the idea, but Simon was the boss, the man with the gold. They started forward slowly.

At the back of the house, beneath the cottonwoods, Campo and Dominguez saw Simon start forward. The Indian said, "Better dismount," doing the same himself, "he's going to rush the house. I'll take the side window, you take the back. Let's get closer."

Dominguez nodded agreement. He took off his sombrero and left it on the pommel of his saddle. Afoot, he and Campo splashed across the creek, approaching the house carefully.

Campo moved off to the left to cover the window on that side of the house and Campo crouched down, quietly levering a round into the breech of his Winchester repeater.

From where he was he could see the three men walking their horses into the yard of the ranch house, see the moonlight gleaming on their weapons.

Then they were out of his sight and he did not see Simon Black swing down from his horse and walk to the door. Forrest had stepped to one side of the door, pistol held beside his head. All hell could break loose when

152

Simon kicked the door in, he knew. He hoped Cameron didn't have a scattergun.

Cummings and Wally had positioned themselves near the two front windows, ready to provide backup or prevent any escape through those windows. If Cameron Black was in there, they had him boxed good and proper. He was a dead man.

Simon Black kicked the door open and the shot rang out.

Wally spun toward the door and crouched . His every sense had anticipated shots from the house and so he turned that way, but even as he did he knew he had made a mistake. The shot had come not from the house, but from behind him. Now before he could spin back or drop to the porch, two bullets punctured his body, the second breaking his spine, and Wally folded up like a rag doll. He tumbled to the porch, rifle flying free, dead.

Abel Packett shifted his sights and aimed at the other man, Cummings, and fired twice more. Both shots missed and the big man had time to fire back, grazing Packett's horse in the chest before the Kid, afoot to Packett's left, fired two shots from the hip and the slugs from the muzzle of the Colt ripped through Cummings's body.

"Got him!" the Kid said and then a .44-40 bullet from Campo's rifle took the top of his head off and the kid jackknifed forward to die in the dust of the yard.

Packett had kicked out of the stirrups of his wounded horse and was now dashing toward the shelter of the barn, shots ringing out as bullets dogged his heels and splintered the wood of the barn door frame. He dove into the barn and positioned himself behind the buckboard, where he opened up, trying to cover Beeman's rush for the barn.

Beeman had rounded the corner of the house to surprise Dominguez, who fired too hastily, his bullet merely clipping Beeman's shoulder.

Beeman's return shot had been truer. His pistol cracked off with deadly thunder and his bullet found the Mexican's heart, flinging him back.

Then Beeman had turned and made his run for the barn, Packett covering him. He tried to run in a zigzag pattern, but it wasn't good enough. Forrest, firing from one knee on the porch, put four rounds into the big man, the last two after Beeman was already dead on the ground.

Forrest raised a triumphant hand toward Simon Black and a bullet from the barn answered the gesture. The round from Packett's rifle passed through the redhead's throat and he sagged into a sitting position, and propped up against the wall, he died.

"Let's go, let's go!" Simon Black yelled as he vaulted the porch rail and rushed toward his horse. A bullet whipped past his head. It might have tagged his hat. Simon didn't stop to look.

Campo had already made the horses and he rode to Simon as the black-eyed man ran trying to escape the constant fire from the barn.

Simon Black swung around on the run and the two remaining members of the gang rode out at a dead gallop. Packett was behind them and so instead of turning back toward town, trying to run the gauntlet of gunfire, they rode on deeper into the hills, toward the west and the sandhills.

Packett, amazingly, hadn't been tagged. He staggered out into the yard, his legs wobbling. He looked around at the carnage, at the remains of his gang, and then slowly, grimly, walked to his horse.

They wouldn't escape. They didn't know the country and even if they found Hollingsworth Pass, they would be below him all the way to the desert.

Methodically he reloaded his rifle, swung onto his horse's back, and rode out of the ranch, knowing he would never see it again.

The bastards, whoever they were, had destroyed his setup, killing his men, making sure he had no hideout. If it was the last thing he ever did, he was going to see that they died.

He rode at an easy lope. He wasn't going to kill his horse. There was time to catch them. He knew these hills, knew the desert as they didn't. He would take it easy. There was no hurry.

There was time for them to die.

"What went wrong, what went wrong?" Simon Black kept repeating as he and Campo—all that was left of his gang—rode through the hills. To their left were moon-glossed sand dunes, to the right red hills, dusted only here and there with blow sand. Ahead the canyon funneled toward what seemed to be a dead-end canyon. "What went wrong?"

"Those hombres from the saloon," Campo said. "I recognized one of them, even in all of that."

"Cameron's friends, I guess . . . but he wasn't there. That damn lousy lying kid!" Simon Black slammed his hand against his horse's neck in frustration.

"The kid wasn't lying," the Delaware said calmly. "He was too scared to lie."

"What now?" Black asked, looking to Campo ear-

155

nestly for help.

"Give it up," Campo said pragmatically. "The man's given us the slip. There's only you and me and we don't know which direction he's gone. He could be anywhere. Pay me off and we'll split up. Me, I've had enough."

"You'd quit on me!" Simon Black said, his voice rising to a shriek.

The Indian shrugged. "What's the sense in this, boss? We could spend years riding around the desert now and never catch his scent. The ambush down south didn't work. Tracking him didn't work. Trying to attack that ranch didn't work. The man's lucky, and now he's gone."

"So that's what I've been paying you for? To quit on me when it gets tough?"

"What the hell good is my pay doing me? What good is it doing Forrest or Dominguez or—"

"Sure, just crawl away. I should have known better than to take a stinkin' Indian on!"

Campo stiffened, but he didn't snap back. What he had told Simon Black was true. If the madman wanted to spend the rest of his life wandering around the desert searching for his brother, let him. While the trail was warm, Campo had nothing against trying to help hunt the man down. Simon's gold was good. But to stick now no longer made sense. Cameron Black had won.

They rode in silence then, Simon Black sulking, Campo more practically wondering if they were riding to a dead end, occasionally letting his thoughts drift to what he could purchase with the gold he had already amassed, which now rode heavily in his saddlebags.

Looking ahead, Campo could now see that the canyon did not dead-end, but appeared to reach a sheer bluff. Below the white-sand desert floor gleamed in the moonlight, but it was perhaps two thousand feet to the valley floor. He turned in his saddle, seeing no pursuit.

He wasn't sure how many of Cameron Black's gang were still alive, how many there had been in the first place. Would they follow? If it had been Campo, he would have followed, but there was no telling. Maybe they had had enough.

Now they were within a hundred yards of the bluff. To their left the hills had grown higher, to their right there was no visible trail through the broken red rock hills. If there were men following, it seemed they had boxed themselves in good and proper.

Reaching the bluff Campo squinted, slowly searching the landform. Down fifty feet or so he thought he saw a trail slanting northward, but he couldn't see where it might have its beginning. Perhaps that had long ago crumbled away and slid to the desert floor below.

It was only guesswork, but noting the outcropping below them which jutted out like a rock awning, Campo thought he had it.

"Seems we can find the head of the trail that way, over the dunes," he said.

Simon Black looked that way. He himself wouldn't have guessed that, but he trusted the Indian's instincts, no matter how angry he was with him, and they had to get out of there.

"Let's give it a try," he muttered, and he followed Campo over the mountainous dunes, riding toward where the Delaware guessed the trail began.

It took half an hour's searching, riding back and forth along the rim of the bluff, but finally Campo exclaimed, "Here it is, boss. It's narrow right here, but you can see it widen out down below. A tough ride in the dark, but we can make it down!"

But Campo was never to make it down. His voice was smothered into a sort of gurgle and when Simon Black glanced that way he saw the arrow through Campo's throat.

The Apaches came up out of the dunes whooping and firing their guns, letting arrows fly in Simon's direction. In panic he emptied his revolver in their direction, giving him a bare moment, as they hit the ground and dove for cover, to heel his horse hard and drive it off into space, down the sheer-sided bluff, following the broken trail as the firing above pursued him.

The trail widened rapidly and then he was under the rocky overhang they had seen earlier, and the horse, sliding and panicked, outdistanced the Apaches who gave chase on foot.

Halfway down the broken trail Simon found a wide spot where he could leap from the horse's back, and, sending it on ahead, he settled in with his Winchester.

The Apaches, coming on a dead run, rounded the bend behind him one by one, and one by one Simon picked them off. They gave it up finally, and half an hour after his last shot, Simon started on, wanting to catch up with his horse, which was nearly to the desert floor when he saw it.

Nervously he mounted, looking back up the trail, but there was no pursuit. He mounted his horse and started northward.

Northward because he had seen the tracks clearly by moonlight. Two horses had gone that way very recently. Two horses—a man and a woman? From what he knew it seemed likely. The kid had said Cameron and a woman were at the house, but there had been no one there when

158

Simon and his gang arrived. They hadn't passed them coming out.

That left the trail along the bluff.

Two riders. One of them had to be Cameron Black.

The other was undoubtedly Susan.

Both of them would die.

Nineteen

The desert was limitless. It spread out to the north and south as far as the eye could see. Ahead Cameron Black could see the dark bulk of the Chocolate Mountains, but no matter how long they rode they seemed to get no nearer. It was as if the mountains were a mirage, receding as they approached.

He was weary, his horse hanging its head. He had long ago quit perspiring. The desert wind whipped off any moisture his body might produce before it had time to cool his skin.

Cassie rode uncomplainingly at his side. He looked to her constantly, wondering at her strength. He could see determination in her eyes and in the set of her mouth. That and happiness. She was free finally and she was riding into the future with the man she loved.

Only once had Cameron tried to apologize. "I'm sorry, Cassie," he had said, "no woman should have to endure this."

"You just be quiet, Cameron Black," she had said with some heat. "Life *is* hard. I've endured before. This time,

I'm enduring because I know at the end of this trail there will be a life I want with the man I want, so don't you dare apologize for having chosen me to ride beside you."

And that settled that.

Cameron uncorked his canteen and drank a swallow of tepid water, handing the canteen to Cassie when he had done so. She too took only a small drink. It was still two days to Boron and the two quarts of remaining water were all they had to sustain them.

The horses, unfortunately, would be suffering unless they came across water in the meantime, which seemed unlikely as Cameron surveyed the unbroken monotony of the long desert. The best they could do was to ocassionally swab out the horses' mouths with a bandanna soaked in water. Sometimes too they dismounted and walked where the sand was not too deep, to conserve the horses' energy. The bay seemed very tired, but for some reason Captain Jack acted as if he were very fresh, as if he shared their anticipation of better things to come.

Cameron was worried. He had said nothing to Cassie yet, but he was worried. Miles to the south he had seen sand rising in lazy clouds. At first he had assumed it was a dust devil moving across the desert floor, but as they drifted farther west, so did the dust cloud. And the wind was blowing eastward.

It may have been nothing, a mule train, a freight wagon heading toward Boron, but with the troubles of the past months haunting him still, he was of no mind to easily dismiss the following dust.

Toward noon they got lucky, finding a muddy pool of water which Cameron tasted, finding it sweet enough for the horses to drink. He loosened the cinches on Captain

Jack and the bay and let them rest.

Cassie came to him and slipped her arm around his waist. They were in dune country once more, the sand rippling out like a white sea for as far as they could see.

"How far is it to Boron?" Cassie asked.

"Tired?"

"A little bit. Mostly it's the thought that when we reach Boron it will all be finally over."

"That may not be true, Cassie," Cameron Black said gravely.

"What do you mean?" she asked in surprise. "Surely you don't think Packett would . . ."

"I don't mean Packett. He can always find someone else to join his gang. He knows we wouldn't say anything to the law; it would implicate both of us. No, I mean the others—those men who are searching for me."

"They must have given up by now," Cassie said. "They would have to be mad to chase you this far."

"Maybe they are mad," Cameron said. "They pursued me all the way to Fortune."

"You're wrong, you have to be," she said, her eyes searching his.

"Probably," Cameron said, yet deep inside the question remained. Would they follow this far?

"Besides, no one could know where we've gone except Packett, and as you say, he still thinks of you as one of the gang. He wouldn't talk."

"That's true. The odds are very long, aren't they?" He turned to her and petted her hair. "I guess I've been on the run so long that my imagination runs away with me."

They gave the horses another ten minutes' rest and then started up out of the hollow in the dunes. The first Indian's shot missed widely, but the bay reared up and

Cameron had to grab its bridle, turning it by force back into the hollow.

By the time he hit the ground he already had his rifle in his hand and he was scrambling up the dune to look out across the desert in the direction from which the shot had come.

He saw nothing.

"Who was it?" Cassie asked. She lay on her belly beside Cameron Black.

"Apaches. I just got a glimpse of him. There'll be others."

"What do they want?"

"Whatever we have. And the water."

"Let me have the rifle. I'm a fair shot, Cameron."

"But you've never shot a man."

"No, but I will if someone is threatening my husband, our future."

Reluctantly he handed the rifle over and drew his Remington .44 revolver. He would have rather had the long gun, but not to give her the rifle would have seemed a kind of mistrust.

His regret was lessened a moment later. An Apache popped up out of the sand and Cassie drilled him through the chest. The Indian fell back with a death scream in his throat. Cameron Black glanced at Cassie, but there was no look of triumph on her face. Her mouth was set, that was all, and she leveled a fresh cartridge into the breech.

Three long minutes passed, the sun beating down on their backs, before the Apaches made a serious attempt at storming their position.

"Look out!" Cameron yelled. "Take the ones on the left."

Five Apaches had begun a charge toward them.

Cameron two-handed his Remington and triggered off. His first shot took an onrushing Indian in the leg and he crumpled up and went down, crawling away. He switched his sights as Cassie fired, hitting another Apache. Cameron fired twice at an attacking Indian, the first shot missing badly, the second finding flesh. The Indian swatted at his shoulder as if at an insect, but blood streamed from it. He dove to the ground and Cameron lost sight of him. He was unable to determine if the man had crawled away, was creeping forward still, or was lying where he had fallen.

"Is that it?" Cassie wanted to know. "Will they be back?"

"I don't know. It may be they'll wait for reinforcements. Or maybe that is all of them, just a small, roving band. All we can do is wait and see."

"After dark . . . ," she said, knowing how easy it would be for the Apaches to approach their position when the sun went down. Perhaps these had just been young warriors, too anxious to win a victory. After talking it over they might very well decide to wait until night fell.

"I know," Cameron said. He ducked as a half dozen shots from the Apache position plowed up the sand around him and Cassie. "I think they want to keep us pinned down until dark and then storm our position."

"What can we do?" she asked. Cassie's heart was in her throat. She would fight, but that didn't mean she wasn't scared. She felt no shame at being frightened. She had heard all the tales, and once seen a woman who had been held captive by the Apaches. She was hardly recognizable as a human being.

"Hold them off. When it's full dark, we're going to ride like hell toward Boron."

They lay there for hour after hour through the heat of the day, the sand beneath them well over a hundred degrees. The heat caused the vision to swim. Ribbons of superheated air rose before their eyes. The dunes seemed to shift and swell.

Once they saw an Apache carelessly expose himself and both of them fired at him, both missing as he vanished into the sand again.

"Well, we know they're still there," Cassie commented.

"Yes." But Cameron had never had much doubt about that. They had too much the Indians wanted for them to give it up: weapons, horses, and the water, vital on the desert. Add to that the fact that Cassie was a woman . . . they wouldn't quit, Cameron Black knew.

"Is there any chance of someone coming by?" Cassie asked hopefully.

"I don't think so. Everyone knows the Apaches are out here. There's the Butterfield line, of course, but it's several miles north of us, and they don't even run a stage every day."

"It's up to us then," Cassie said with determination.

"It's up to us."

The hours passed with slow monotony, but when the sun did begin to fade, the sky above the mountains to color, Cameron felt his pulse quicken, his heart begin to pound harder. Now whatever was going to happen would happen. They would make good their escape or die on the lonesome desert.

"When?" Cassie asked, looking to the western skies.

"Pretty soon."

"They'll have put men all around us, won't they, so we can't escape?"

"That's right. We'll probably have to ride through some Apaches."

"I wonder how many there are, if they were reinforced."

"We'll find out, I'm afraid," Cameron said. "We're going to go due north, Cassie, toward the Butterfield trail and then into Boron. When we take off we're going to go east for a quarter mile or so and then swing north. That may shake them. I don't think they'll expect us to go east since we were going west when they picked up our trail. If they have men posted out there, that should be the thinnest area."

"All right," Cassie answered. She had trust in her man, and if he thought that was the way to go, she certainly wasn't going to argue or debate his decision.

The day was falling rapidly to purple dusk. There was barely enough light to see by. To Cassie's surprise, Cameron began to fire at the Apaches' position, methodically emptying his pistol, reloading from his belt loops and emptying it again, his shots spaced wide apart, aimed at nothing.

He caught her glance as he reloaded again and he smiled.

"Aren't you wasting ammunition?"

"Sure, but if we make a run for it, we won't need much. We'll either break through or we won't. At least they know we're still here and we still have teeth. It will make them more cautious, make them hold back just a little, and a little time is all we need."

"When do we go?" she asked tremulously.

"Now," he said. "We go now."

He rolled toward her and held her tightly, kissing her deeply for a long moment. Then he nodded and they

166

scooted back down the dune, moving through the near darkness toward the horses.

It was time. Cameron took a deep breath. It wouldn't be only a race for survival, but a run toward the future, where he and Cassie could live together normally, without fear and anxiety. It was a battle that had to be fought so that they could find happiness.

But first they had to survive.

Cameron Black swung aboard Captain Jack, and with his revolver already cocked, heeled the big buckskin savagely and burst up out of the hollow, riding to the east as the war whoops and the roar of guns followed them.

Twenty

The Apache loomed up in front of the big buckskin, grabbing for the bridle, and Cameron let Captain Jack trample him into the sand. The second one was smarter. He was on one knee and he fired from that position. The bullet whipped past Cameron's head and he returned the fire, putting three shots through the barrel of the Remington as fast as it would fire. The Apache remained upright for an impossible length of time and then simply tilted over, dead.

Then they were riding free on the desert, racing eastward. Cameron looked over his shoulder, the powder-heated pistol still in his hand, cocked and ready, but there was no horse pursuit, and if they were chasing them on foot, they were bound to lose.

He wheeled northward after awhile, Cassie, aware of the plan, following him instantly. They ran the horses until Cameron could feel Captain Jack's great strength waning, then they slowed to a gallop, and finally to a walk. They had won. They had beaten the outlaws and the elements, the Apaches and the stalkers who had shadowed Cameron Black.

They had won.

Simon Black rode on through the desert night. He didn't know the area well, but he knew there was only one small town nearby—Boron.

If Cameron had an eventual destination in mind, Simon couldn't guess what it might be; he only knew that it would be necessary for him to stop for provisions and water at Boron.

Simon had long since lost the tracks of the two horses in the blow sand on the desert, but that didn't matter. It was Boron where Cameron would be stopping with his whore.

The stars were bright in the clear desert sky, the moon rising. The silver dunes gave way finally to a red sand desert where the footing was easier for the horse, the hardpan only inches below the surface.

Simon had spent long hours in the saddle. The day had been excruciatingly hot and dry, but he had minded none of it. He was confident now, certain of Cameron's intended goal. He knew, of course, that there were Apaches out there somewhere, but he had no fear of them. Fate had dictated that he would find Cameron Black and finally destroy him. He even whistled as he rode despite the fact that his lips were dry and cracked from the desert heat.

It was there—a Mecca dimly lit, promising, nearly spiritual. Cameron Black, riding the leg-weary buckskin, felt the horse's energy rise as his own spirits lifted.

Cassie's hand found his. The lights of Boron gleamed dully against the black horizon.

"There," she said. "It exists. The world exists. Promise and the future."

Cameron shared her nearly mystical thrill. After the desert, all that had gone before, a town where people lived and worked and grew sick and had children, was nearly startling. It was as if reality had become unreality. Now, the sight of lights, the knowledge that it was a real town they were riding into and not some desert mirage, was overpowering in some inexplicable way. They would have a hotel, a stable, a restaurant, a church. . . .

Without meaning to, both of them lifted their horses to a quicker pace until they were running side by side and Cameron Black let loose with a Texas yell, joyous and unrestrained.

Reaching the city limits they slowed and walked their weary horses through the street. Cameron spotted a boy, barefoot and ragged, and asked him, "Where's the preacher live, boy?"

The kid gawked at him but pointed. "Second Street. Turn south on it. Third house, the yellow one."

To his surprise, Cameron tossed a silver dollar to the kid. Cameron Black turned to Cassie and asked, "Have you changed your mind, lady?"

"What do you think?"

"Then it's Second Street," he said, and they rode up the main thoroughfare of Boron until they saw the painted sign marking it.

The preacher was in his nightshirt, half asleep. Perhaps because it was late he began a lecture. "I don't know if you young people have considered all of the ramifications of marriage, its obligations and meanings . . ."

Cameron Black slipped the preacher a gold double-eagle and said, "We've considered it all, Reverend."

Cassie managed to keep from laughing; still she was nervous. She had never been married before. Could she make this man happy? She worried about that briefly until Cameron Black took her hand and hugged her tightly; then she knew. She had given him a gift that meant much to him: her love.

Neither of them had thought of a ring. The parson's wife, a lady of fifty with sagging jowls and kind eyes, loaned them hers for the ceremony.

The preacher's voice seemed to drone on interminably, but the entire ceremony couldn't have lasted more than ten minutes. When they stepped outside again to stand beneath the canopy of stars both Cameron and Cassie felt stunned, as if there was no reality to the moment, and yet Cameron held in his hand the proof that it had really happened.

"We're really free, we're really married," Cassie said in wonder.

"Yes." Cameron didn't hug her or kiss her. He only held her hand and stood with her until with sudden high spirits, he tugged her forward. "Come on," he said.

"Where to?"

"Just come along, *wife.*"

He half dragged her across the street and then up the block until they found the jeweler's. The man who owned the store lived upstairs. He came down in his nightshirt, grousing and holding his back. But he was still ready to do business when he saw the coins in Cameron's hand.

"What is it?" he asked, forcing a sleepy smile.

"A wedding ring. What will you have, Cassie?" Cameron asked.

"Plain gold. Gold that endures and shines as brightly on the day I die as it does now."

The jeweler showed her his plain bands and she picked one in her size. Very plain, very beautiful, and Cameron Black overpaid the jeweler.

"And now it's done," Cameron Black said as they went back out into the warm, dry desert night.

"And now," Cassie corrected, "it begins."

They hired a boy to have their horses put up at the stable, and walked, arm in arm, oblivious of the rest of the town, the rest of the world, to their hotel, where Cameron registered proudly: Mr. & Mrs. Cameron Black.

The room was small, clean, the window opened so that the desert breeze fluttered the curtains softly and cooled the room.

They lay back, fully dressed, and for a long while simply wondered at the luck that had finally come their way and brought them to this moment.

Simon Black's horse was worn to the nub. It staggered into Boron, past the raucous saloons, the shuttered general store, the dark and empty saddlery. None of these held any interest for Simon Black.

It was to the stable he went first. There he asked the stable hand, "Anybody new in tonight? I'm supposed to meet my brother here."

"Several. What was he riding?"

"I'm not sure. He's liable to cut anything out of the remuda."

172

"Carl!" the stable man barked, and the kid who had been dozing in a stall poked his head up. "Who come in tonight?"

"Old man Stallings. Then Mr. Rose. Then two strangers. Never seen 'em before. Man and a woman. They went to Preacher Brown's."

"Then where?" Simon asked.

"Got no idea, mister. They asked me to park their horses and I did. That's them, the buckskin and the bay."

Without another word Simon Black turned and walked from the stable. He knew where Cameron would be, had to be—the nearest hotel. Where else would a man go on his wedding night?

I hope you've enjoyed it, Cameron, brother, because it's the last night you'll spend with her, he thought, and he walked up the street, leaving his own horse unattended.

They lay together on the lumpy hotel bed, awake as they dreamed, hands interlaced. Through the parted curtains of the window Cameron Black could see the stars, brilliant in the summer sky.

"From here?" Cassie asked her husband.

"California, I suppose. We'll sell the horses and take the stage out to Sacramento. I'll feel bad about leaving Captain Jack, but in a way we're better off without any vestige of the past. We'll see if we like it, if I can find decent work. I've got a little money left, so we may even be able to buy some land and go to ranching on a small scale. We'll have to see. If we don't care for it, we'll move on."

"All right," Cassie said. She rolled her head toward

173

Cameron Black. "It seems so strange, but so fulfilling to have someone you know will be there in the morning, and in the evening, someone who will always stand with you."

"Funny, isn't it," Cameron said, "that we both waited this long instead of making a mistake we would have regretted the rest of our lives."

She rolled to him and snuggled against him, her hand on his chest, her face against his throat, and he lay back, his eyes closed, his body totally at peace.

The boot slammed against the latch of the door and it swung open violently.

Simon Black stepped into the room, his gun leveled.

Cameron looked toward the chair five feet away where his gun hung in its holster and then back at the intruder, his mind finding slow recognition.

"Simon!"

"Yeah, it's me Cameron."

"What in hell are you doing here? With a gun? Cassie, this is my brother, Simon." He started to rise, but the black-eyed man cocked his Colt and aimed it. His voice was more than menacing.

"Stay where you are, Cameron, I'm warning you."

"Simon? What in hell's the matter with you?" Cameron Black asked. He squeezed Cassie's hand and then let go. "I just got married. Why didn't you let me know you were here? I could've used a best man."

"Funny, Cameron, laughable. Who are you trying to kid? You can't talk your way out of this one."

"Simon, what the hell is going on?" He noticed now the slightly mad look in Simon Black's eyes. His brother was trail-dusty, gaunt. He had a haunted look about him. "Sit down, Simon, relax awhile and tell me what's

174

troubling you."

"Relax!" Simon fell into a fit of laughter which lasted far too long. "Listen," he said, like a man suddenly sober, "I haven't come this far to relax, I've come to kill you.

"Those fools I hired botched the job at every opportunity. I promise you I won't botch it. Your gang, mine, they're all dead. Shot each other to pieces up in Fortune. But you're still alive, Cameron—for now. I mean to remedy that."

"Simon . . . what are you talking about?"

"As if you didn't know. I know you saw me. I know you would have killed me if I didn't kill you first. I have to do it now. You and this whore of yours. I'm not going to hang."

"Simon! I don't know what you're talking about."

"That night. I know you saw me. The flames were bright. That's why I took off. I knew you'd follow, and you finally found out where I was. You and Susan. Why did she want you? I was there. I would have been good to her. But she had to want you. Why, Cameron?"

"*You!* You're the one who killed Susan and her parents? You're the one who set fire to her house?"

"As if you didn't know."

"Simon—I never saw you. I didn't recognize the man who rode past me in the dark. All of this was for nothing."

Simon Black stood staring at his brother. "For nothing . . ." he mumbled. Then he became suddenly alert. "But it doesn't matter now, does it—now that you know? You'll kill me or have me arrested and hung. You still have to die Cameron."

And he raised his gun, aiming deliberately as Cameron prepared for one desperate lunge toward his gun, knowing he would never make it.

The gunshot was loud in the small room and Cameron saw Simon buckle at the knees. The man in the doorway had drilled him through the spine, but still Simon Black had time to turn and return the fire, and Abel Packett took a bullet through the chest and slumped against the door frame.

Simon was on the floor, dying. Packett was pale, the blood flowing from his wound.

"Nobody shoots my people, nobody. You were a good man, Black. You . . ." And then Packett fell onto his side to lie there, dead.

Crowds of people filled the hallway, gawking at the two dead men. The hotel manager squeezed through the mob to survey the damage and look at Cameron Black.

"What happened here?" he asked.

"I don't know. Two men with a grudge. They chose our room to finish it in. My wife and I would like another room, please."

"Yes, certainly," the manager agreed quickly.

Cameron asked him, "Is the Butterfield stage office open evenings?"

"Why, yes. Why do you ask? I hope this tragedy hasn't given you a bad impression of Boron."

"No," Cameron Black answered, "it's not that. My wife and I have been planning on traveling on. California. I think. Sacramento."

"You have something waiting for you out there?" the hotel manager asked.

"Yes. I think we do. A whole new world."